I0633251

THE FRENCH KILLING

The D.C. Man Series

Top Secret Kill

Search & Destroy

Your Daughter Will Die!

The French Killing

THE FRENCH KILLING

PETER ROHRBACH
WRITING AS "JAMES P. CODY"

BRASH
BOOKS

Copyright © 2024 The Estate of Peter Rohrbach

For Sheila, in recollection of happy days together in Paris.

The characters and events portrayed in this book are fictitious. Any similarity to real persons, living or dead, is coincidental and not intended by the author.
No part of this book may be reproduced, or stored in a retrieval system, or transmitted in any form or by any means, electronic, mechanical, photocopying, recording, or otherwise, without express written permission of the publisher.

ISBN-13: 978-1-954841-94-9

Published by
Brash Books
PO Box 8212
Calabasas, CA 91372
www.brash-books.com

PUBLISHER'S NOTE

James P. Cody was the pseudonym of Peter T. Rohrbach, a former Catholic priest of the Carmelite Order who lived, prayed and served in a Washington D.C. rectory until he left the priesthood in 1966. Rohrbach wrote the first book in the *D.C. Man* series, *Top Secret Kill*, as a side project while he was a priest. He wrote the three subsequent novels in the series after he left the priesthood.

To further confuse things, the name that Rohrbach was given at birth was actually James Cody. During his childhood, his parents died and he was adopted by the Rohrbach family and took their last name. But when he joined the priesthood, he changed first name from "James" to "Peter Thomas."

The French Killing was originally published in 1975. The details about Rohrback / Cody and the series were first revealed by Tom Simon on the *Paperback Warrior* blog in 2018. The popular article had the unintended effect of making copies of the original paperbacks scarce and expensive... until the publication of these new editions on the 50th Anniversary of the original series publication.

CHAPTER ONE

She was waiting for me in my outer office when I arrived.

Quite attractive, probably somewhere in her early thirties, and she seemed to have everything packaged together rather nicely—a trim figure, advantageously displayed in a pale beige suit, carefully brushed blonde hair, perfectly manicured nails. And her skirt had hiked up slightly along her thighs, enabling me to see a fine pair of long silky legs.

I thought....

There were some imperfections to the picture. Those legs, for instance. They were long and graceful, yes, but there was a trace of a bit too much muscle in them, as if she had trained as a dancer or had engaged in a lot of athletic activity over the years. Even more significant were the eyes. They were gray and frosty, and they suggested an excessive control and impassivity; they seemed to say that she was a woman who was always in complete charge of the situation and who couldn't be manipulated in any way. Everyone to his own taste, but I like my girls a little more soft and pliant.

I didn't know who she was, and I was startled to find her sitting there when I entered my office about ten thirty that August morning. However, she seemed to know who I was, and when our eyes met she nodded her head slightly in greeting. Annie, my secretary, who had been seated at her desk at the other side of the room, was now on her feet and moving toward the door of my private office so she could hold it open for me to pass by.

If I had known that this woman was waiting for me, I would have used the other door down the corridor, which gives me immediate access to my private office without having to pass through the outer office. But then, I hardly expected to find any clients sitting out there these days. Brian Petersen, registered lobbyist, just wasn't doing a tremendous amount of work in the lobbying profession on Capitol Hill any more.

And now, in retrospect, there was another thing I should have done differently that morning. I should have refused to see her. I should have told Annie to get her the hell out of my office. I didn't know it then, but she was big trouble: In the next few days, she was going to involve my already battered life in a series of tragic killings and violence.

Annie closed the door behind me, and when I nodded my head toward the outer office, told me: "A Mademoiselle Therese Ballard."

"French?" I asked.

"Veddy French. Veddy sexy voice. Deep and throaty, you know."

"What the hell does she want?"

"She's from the French Embassy, but, of course, she wouldn't tell a poor laborer like me the nature of her business. But she simply had to see Monsieur Petersen. It's *très important*."

"My God, she didn't say *trés important,* did she?"

Annie smiled softly. "Well, no. I'm dramatizing it a bit. But she said she simply had to see you, and she would just wait here until you came in."

"Oh, my. I don't know…."

"I've also placed a call for you to Senator Phillips' office. You know, Brian, you've got to get that material about the strip-mining up to the Hill, and I thought Senator Phillips would be a good man to contact."

"Oh, yeah, Hank Phillips would help, I guess." The strip-mining stuff was some material that had been forwarded to me by a small client of mine from West Virginia, and my task as a lobbyist was to get the information to some responsive and powerful ears in the Congress. But I seemed to have lost enthusiasm for that kind of work, and it was Annie who kept prodding me along, making sure that I at least did some lobbying these days.

"And what about Joan of Arc out there?" Annie asked.

I took a deep breath, and ran my hand across my face. I wasn't in one of my better moods that day. The previous evening I had had dinner with an old friend of mine from the West Coast, a pal who had played football with me at UCLA and was in town for the day on business. During our dinner we had talked about the old days at college, carefully avoiding the problems of my later years, but when I returned home after dinner I couldn't help ruminating over these past few years in Washington. And that always puts me in a frightfully lousy mood.

"I don't know if I'm interested in talking to anybody from the French Embassy today," I said. But when Annie looked at me reproachfully I finally said: "All right. Send her in. I guess I can at least listen to her *très important* story."

"You are very kind to see me at such short notice, Monsieur Petersen," said Therese Ballard in her French accent. She was seated across the desk from me, her legs crossed, and those long thighs slightly exposed again. "But it was quite urgent, and Monsieur Duval from our embassy staff recommended you. He said you have helped us before."

"Oh, in just a few little things. Nothing significant."

"Nevertheless. He said you were the person to contact. Does the name Georges Hervé mean anything to you?"

"Not a thing, Mademoiselle."

"Nor to most other people, either. Apart from the international financial community, that is. He is probably one of Europe's most important financiers—not in the class of a Rothschild perhaps, but extremely important nevertheless. However, he detests publicity of any kind. He never grants interviews, and his name rarely appears in the newspapers, and he travels quietly and inconspicuously."

"I can't blame him. Publicity can ruin your life."

"Perhaps. But it complicates our problem now. You see, Monsieur Hervé will be arriving at Dulles Airport tomorrow night on an extremely important financial mission. It has no direct connection with the embassy, since it is a purely mercantile matter, and in fact, Monsieur Hervé, following his usual custom, will not even visit the embassy. But we at the embassy are concerned about his safety in Washington."

"Some kind of a threat against his life?"

"No, nothing like that. But our people in France are worried about the newspaper stories about the crime and violence on the streets of Washington, and we want to make sure he is adequately protected."

"Oh, those stories are exaggerated. Sure, there's crime and violence in D.C., but so is there everywhere else. One would think twice, for instance, before walking through certain sections of Paris."

"Yes, I suppose you're right, but you know how rumors can fly and how apprehensive people can become far away. But our government is most interested in the success of his venture, and the embassy wants to guarantee his complete safety during his brief stay in your capital."

"Seems simple enough. Get the D.C. police to ferry him around. Or, if he's all that important, get the Executive Protection Service or even the Secret Service. Have the ambassador call the White House."

"But, don't you see, that's the problem. Monsieur Hervé absolutely refuses to have any official protection. He claims it is unnecessary, and it will only draw attention to him. And attention is what he desperately tries to avoid. In Paris, we suggested that some of our people from the embassy escort him around, but he furiously rejected that. Monsieur Hervé is a very determined and self-reliant man."

"There's another answer, then. If you're concerned about his safety you can employ a good detective agency here in D.C., and have them put an umbrella around him from a distance. They'll be able to keep an eye on him, and watch out for his safety, and he wouldn't even know about it."

"That's precisely what we want, Monsieur Petersen. And that's why we came to you."

"But, Mademoiselle, I'm not a detective agency, I'm a lobbyist."

"Of course. But we also know that you perform discreet services for special clients. We thought you could put this—how do you say?—package together for us. You know the good people in Washington, and you could supervise this project for us by getting people who would insure Monsieur Hervé's safety during his visit."

I started to protest, but I stopped. There was no sense playing coy with the French gal. If Duval from the embassy had recommended her to me, she obviously knew the story about Brian Petersen. And it wasn't particularly pretty.

I know, only too well, what Duval must have told her: About two years ago Petersen landed back in town, Duval would say, following a six months absence when he had fled Washington after a big personal tragedy. But he had changed, and the fire and drive seemed to have gone out of him. Oh, he opened a lobbying office again, but it wasn't the same as a few years earlier when he was the golden young man of Washington lobbyists. He seemed to be just going through the motions, picking up a few small clients, working for them desultorily. It appeared as if he were about to throw it all over again and take off once more.

But then, he started somehow to get into those discreet services for some of his clients. First, it was cleaning up a little blackmail operation, and then plugging a leak in a Senate committee. But, as his reputation spread, the assignments became more complicated and more dangerous, everything from unraveling a murder to that messy Ellen Rankin kidnaping last spring. Petersen continued his lobbying operation, but more and more of his time seemed to be spent on these other activities. And people came to him for help—small people, and even the powers of Washington. They knew he could get that necessary job done. He had excellent credentials: Petersen is a former college football player who has done a tour in Army Intelligence in Europe, the son-in-law of a former U.S. senator, and an experienced lobbyist who really knows his way around this complicated government town. And, now that his life had fallen apart, he was willing to do that tough job for you; he just didn't seem to give a damn any more. He could fight and he could shoot, and he would do both of them if he had to.

There was a market for such services in Washington. Sometimes the ordinary machinery, with all the attendant publicity, just wouldn't suffice, and they had to turn to someone like Petersen, someone who had the know-how and someone who could be discreet. Sure, he'd do the job, and he'd keep his mouth shut. He wouldn't do anything blatantly dishonest, but he was willing to skirt the law for you if he felt you were getting a dirty deal and had no other recourse. However, he was no knight in shining white armor; he'd make you pay for his services, and pay well.

I realized that Therese Ballard undoubtedly knew all that. She was also probably wondering why I had drifted into this kind of operation. Well, I wondered about it, too. I don't really know, but it did give me something to do that got my juices flowing again for a short while. And my juices don't flow much any more. But there was one thing she probably didn't know: I'm very selective about my clients, and I pick and choose very carefully among them.

And I didn't want this one.

I suppose part of the reason was the dour mood I had gotten myself into as the result of those long, late-hour reminiscences last night. Furthermore, the assignment didn't interest me. It was too routine, without any challenge. A lot of people around town could do this job for her. Let her get somebody else.

"I'm sorry," I told her, "I'm not interested."

She was carrying a black leather purse strung around her shoulder with a long strap, and now she opened it and pulled out an envelope. Sliding it across the desk to me, she said, "That might indicate how important this task is to us."

I opened the envelope, and withdrew a check, a cashier's check made out by the Riggs Bank for the sum of ten thousand dollars. "I'm sorry," I said, shaking my head no.

"Of course, we are always willing to add more to that if you find you have additional expenses."

"That's not the point——" I started, but at that moment Annie buzzed me on the intercom and told me she had Senator Phillips on the line. I didn't want to talk to Phillips in front of the Ballard woman, and so I excused myself to go out to Annie's office and take the call there.

My conversation with Hank Phillips was brief and friendly. And frank. I told him I needed assistance in getting some material about strip-mining into the proper hands, and he agreed to help. We made a date to meet for lunch the following day. When I hung up the phone, I slowly lighted a cigarette.

"How's it going with Joan of Arc?" asked Annie.

"No big deal. She wants me to put together a package to make sure some important visiting Frenchman doesn't get bopped on the head during his stay in D.C."

"Why, is he in some danger?"

"No, they've just got the jitters about crime on the streets. And they've offered me ten thou to arrange it."

"Great!"

"But I'm refusing it."

Annie studied my face, looking for some reason for the refusal of such easy money, but then she looked away. She knew she wouldn't find any simple answers for the peculiar things that Brian Petersen sometimes does. Instead, she pulled open a desk drawer, and extracted the office ledger. "As I read this," she said, "We've been having very little money coming in here the last few months, and our debts are exceeding our credits. You know, we have to take care of such mundane little things as office rent."

She was right, of course. I hadn't been doing much since last spring at all. After that Rankin affair, I felt whipped, and indeed all of my wounds still haven't healed completely. I had been loafing most of the summer, showing up at the office every day for a few hours, but spending most of my afternoons out at Burning Tree playing golf.

"Oh, my," I said, and returned to my private office.

Therese Ballard had also marshaled her arguments in my brief absence. Without waiting for me to say anything, she said immediately, "Monsieur Duval at the embassy was most sure you would help us."

She had found the right button to push. I had done some favors for Duval and Duval had done some favors for me. But, if my memory served me correctly, he was at least one up on me, and I owed him one now. And that was the way the game was played in Washington—you've got to keep returning favors to keep the score even. If you don't, then you don't survive in this jungle of a town.

I sat down behind my desk, paused for a moment and listened to the traffic below on Connecticut Avenue, then took a deep drag on my cigarette. What the hell, I thought. It's easy money, and I'm not doing anything, anyway.

"All right," I said, "I'll take the assignment."

I picked up the check for ten thousand, and folded it carefully in two.

"I'll need some details," I told Therese Ballard as I reached for a pencil.

"I'm afraid there aren't too many details to tell about Monsieur Hervé. He always tries to remain as inconspicuous as possible. He will arrive at Dulles tomorrow afternoon at four o'clock on Air France Flight 203."

"Traveling under his own name?"

"Oh, of course. There is no need to assume another name for the trip, since his name is so little known. But you cannot miss him. He is a short dark man with a mustache. He is in his early fifties. He walks very erect and briskly, and he usually wears dark, conservative clothes, and most often a homburg. We think he will be staying at the Mayflower Hotel."

"How long?"

"Only a few days. Perhaps two days. He is then scheduled to go on to New York."

"Aren't you afraid about his safety in New York?" I said dryly.

"As we understand it, he will only meet some people in JFK, and then he will fly directly back to Paris. It is here in Washington that his business will take place, and that is why our people are apprehensive. His business negotiations in this endeavor are highly critical for the stability of the French economy, and perhaps for the economy of a number of nations in the free world."

"Okay. I'll get some good people to pick him up at the airport, and then shadow him around town so that he doesn't get mugged or anything."

"And, as you suggested, Monsieur Petersen, it would be most advisable if Monsieur Hervé were not aware that we were taking these precautionary measures. If he learned that the embassy was guarding him, he would be displeased."

"That can be done, I suppose. But it will make the job a bit more difficult. It would certainly be helpful if we could know his schedule in advance. Places where he's going, things like that."

"I'm sure it would. But I'm also sure a man of your competence can arrange to protect Monsieur Hervé without his realizing it. We mustn't upset Monsieur Hervé, you know."

"No, we musn't upset Monsieur Hervé," I said with a touch of irony, but Therese Ballard didn't seem to notice the tone in my voice.

"One final thing," she said. "We would like to do this in the usual way. The embassy wants no official connection with this operation, and we ask you not to reveal your employer. And, of course, you will not contact the embassy. We will contact you."

That indeed was the usual procedure. These assignments were ordinarily contracted by people on the lower embassy level—people like Duval or this Ballard woman—so that the ambassador would have no official connection with the operation. And, in a city that is so terrified of bugged telephones, they didn't want me calling into the embassy. They would deal with people like Brian Petersen, but they didn't want anybody to know about it. That was okay with me. The hell with them. I'll just do the job, and take their money.

Therese Ballard was on her feet now, and I walked around the desk to escort her from the office. She was taller than I had first realized, somewhere around five-seven, and with her high heels she made a good partner for my six-foot-two height. She paused and laid her hand on my arm, and I could smell the heady odor of excellent French perfume. She was standing fairly close to me now, and I didn't know what all that meant. A little dash of Gallic charm perhaps to cement the deal? It was all quite futile, because I felt myself curiously unmoved.

"*Bonne chance,*" she said. "We will be in contact with you."

"Sure. Give my regards to Duval."

"*Certainement.*"

After she had departed I could still smell the lingering odor of that perfume. I shook my head and walked out to Annie's office, and placed the check on her desk without any comment.

"Thank God," she said. "I'm going to deposit this right away before you change your mind."

I went back into my office, and glanced at the pad on which I had scratched the few items Ballard had given me about the visiting Frenchman. It looked like a pretty simple deal, and I couldn't get myself very excited about it. I pushed the pad away, leaned back in my chair, and closed my eyes.

Some weeks later I re-read those same notes again, and I was amazed that I hadn't seen the flaws at the time. Perhaps it was because of my real disinterestedness in the whole assignment, or perhaps my lethargic mood had clouded my reasoning processes, making me gullible and unobservant. At any rate, Therese Ballard had very neatly and very easily taken me in.

She had set me up quite cleverly as her patsy for a French killing.

CHAPTER TWO

I had lunch that day with some friends at Paul Young's restaurant on Connecticut Avenue, and then went back to my office again in the afternoon, a rare occurrence for me these recent months.

I could see the surprise on Annie's face when I walked in. "I've got to get to work on that French thing," I told her.

"You'd better," she answered. "I've already deposited the check."

I chuckled, and went into my office. Annie was one of the few good things that had happened to me since my return to Washington. When I was trying to set up this office again she had answered an ad, and she seemed perfect for what I needed. A suburban housewife with two school-age children, she wanted to return to work and supplement her husband's income. I only needed some part-time help to get started again, and as it turned out, that was all I ever needed. Thus, Annie was able to come in about nine in the morning, and leave about two thirty in the afternoon before her children returned from school. She ran the office efficiently and expertly for me, but in addition to that she had become over the past two years a close friend. She was one of the few points of stability in my floundering life.

I sat behind my desk, lighted a cigarette, and started to give some thought to the protection of the visiting Frenchman, but I think I knew from the outset what I would do. I lifted the phone and placed a call to Tom Ferris, and a few seconds later he came on the line.

"I've got some business for you, Tom," I said.

"Yeah, Brian?" he said guardedly. Tom wasn't in any need of new business these days, I knew, and he only accepted assignments from old friends like me. "What is it?" he asked.

"I'm trying to locate Judge Crater."

He laughed. "Try dredging the deep, deep sea. The corpse with the concrete shoes is Judge Crater."

I then proceeded to outline the assignment the Ballard woman had given me that morning; I told Tom that we had to protect this Hervé fellow without letting him know he was being protected.

"What is this Hervé," Tom asked, "some kind of a nut?"

"He's probably got more sense than the embassy people who are all jittery about his safety in town. But they want to pay good money, and they don't want to ruffle his feathers."

"It's doing it the hard way. If we could just stick a couple of bodyguards with him and escort him around town, then it would be a snap. Or, even if we knew his schedule, we could stake out men along the way. But this way, dammit, we need a lot of operatives. Men in front of him, men behind him, lots of cars, radios, the whole bit. It gets to be a damn complicated operation, Brian."

"Don't worry about the expense, Tom. I've got lots of money up front, and if that isn't enough. I can get more. We'll both make an easy piece of change."

"But it seems so unnecessarily involved. Why can't I just have a couple of men meet this Hervé at Dulles tomorrow, introduce themselves, and then squire him around?"

"Because that isn't the way our client wants it. And I know you can do it, Tom."

"Yeah," he said slowly, "I guess I can."

And I knew he could. Tom Ferris ran one of the best, if not *the* best, private detective organizations in town. He was a former special agent in the FBI back in the J. Edgar Hoover days, but after about ten years he one day suddenly and inexplicably quit. Tom doesn't talk much about the reasons for his impulsive decision to resign and forfeit a lot of retirement benefits, but one night when he and I were drinking late he did say to me: "You know, Brian, I just couldn't take it any more—the old man was becoming a real fascist." However, Tom prospered in his own firm, and he now has the reputation of a deadly honest, extremely efficient private detective. He has complained to me that practically all of his work is quite routine—surveillance, protection, investigation—but he does it well. And he retains a low profile. You won't even find his number listed in the phone directory, and he never advertises his services. But old Washington hands like me know that Tom is the man to get when you need some good professional surveillance work done.

"Okay," Tom said. "Let me get to work on this. I'll organize a program, and get some men together. I'll call you back later this afternoon or evening, and let you know what I've set up."

Annie came in to say good-by for the day, and I sat there alone in the office for a little while, smoking a cigarette. Since there seemed to be nothing else to do that day, I finally closed the office and took the elevator down to the garage in the basement. I retrieved my Oldsmobile, and started my trek over to Virginia before the rush-hour traffic got going. After I had crossed the Potomac on the 14th Street Bridge I got on Route 1 toward Arlington, then took a sharp right to the plateau where my house is located. It's a red-brick structure with Norman trim, built on the edge of the plateau, and the lower level has a good-sized swimming pool and a fantastic view of the Washington skyline across the river.

The house was, of course, empty.

I went down to the bar in the family room and mixed myself a quick Gibson, and after I had taken a few sips of it I kicked off my trousers and changed into a pair of swimming trunks. Sliding open the glass doors, I stepped out to the patio and looked at the clear water in the pool, which was now shimmering in the late-afternoon heat of that August day.

The water was warm, but nevertheless it felt invigorating, and I lapped the pool six times before I pulled up at the edge and lifted myself over onto the concrete apron. My wind was still good, despite the half-pack of cigarettes I smoked each day and the hours I spent in downtown Washington. I returned to the family room, gathered up my drink, and picked up the phone.

"Hello," I said when it was finally answered. "I just got home a few minutes ago."

"It must have been hot in the city," she said. I could hear the sound of children's voices in the background.

"Another scorcher. This is our night for dinner, isn't it?"

"It sure is. I've got something great for you. Have a drink for yourself, because it'll take me an hour to get these kids fed and settled down."

"Take your time. I'm in no hurry." I smiled faintly as I hung up the phone. Joyce, who lived about ten minutes away, was a thirtyish divorcee, left with three young children. She came over about every two or three weeks to cook supper for me, and there was nothing maternal about her ministrations to me.

I finished my drink and walked back into the spacious laundry room, which I had outfitted with gym equipment—some mats and rings and horses, a punching bag, and one of those bicycle things that grind away in a stationary position. I worked out for about half an hour, my daily routine—doing sit-ups, chinning myself on the rings, lifting myself over the horses. I punched the bag for awhile and ended up with a fast run on the bicycle. In addition to keeping myself in shape, I enjoy doing those demanding calisthenics each day. It's something you can do unthinkingly, and there's some strange catharsis for me in punishing my body this way. I was covered with perspiration when I finished, and I walked down to the bathroom at the end of the hall where I took a shower, lukewarm at first but then gradually cooler until I ended up with an ice-cold shower. As I toweled myself off, I told myself that the old body, despite all its mistreatment, was still in good shape. I kept my weight at an even two hundred ten now, and it was adequately distributed over my six-two frame. I have dark hair, which I keep closely cropped, just enough so that I can comb it; and people tell me that, with my gray eyes and even features, I look fairly handsome. Maybe. I don't know. I do know, however, that even if the outside of the package looks pretty good, the inside is no bargain at all.

I changed into powder-blue slacks and a white shirt open at the collar, and made myself another drink while waiting for Joyce to arrive. She appeared a few minutes later, carrying an oblong pan covered with a towel.

"Something special," she said. "Shish kebab." She deposited the pan on the bar and pulled off the towel so that I could inspect the skewered pieces of lamb and various vegetables.

"Why don't we barbecue it outside?" I asked, and when she agreed we carried it out to my portable barbecue cooker near the edge of the pool. After we had dumped some charcoal in the contraption and ignited it, we sat on the far side of the pool and watched the flames leap up and then simmer down as the charcoal turned to gray ash. I had made a Manhattan for Joyce and refreshed my own Gibson, and it was pleasant sitting there in the early evening with this attractive woman. Joyce was ash blonde and trim, and she now displayed her fine figure to good advantage in a set of white hip-huggers and a halter blouse that exposed her flat stomach. I had known her for about five years now; in fact, when I first met her she was still married to her husband. The young Virginia matron, very much involved in all the things that young matrons tend to get into—the garden clubs, the civic activities, the frequent entertaining. Then, the whole thing blew up for her, and it was a lousy deal. She had married when her husband was still in college, and she had helped support him through school by working as a secretary, full-time at first and later part-time after the first child came. Hubby—whom I never really liked, anyway—obtained a fairly good job in the government, but after a few promotions and two more children he got itchy pants or something and decided to call it quits on the marriage. Great gratitude there. A divorce followed and regular alimony payments, but that's all Joyce had left.

Except for an occasional evening with an equally bruised chap named Brian Petersen. We were good for each other, though. Neither of us demanded or expected too much of the other. *Indeed,* neither of us demanded or expected too much of anything. Two of life's walking wounded.

We took the shish kebab into the air-conditioned house to eat it, and I broke out a little red wine. A good meal. We washed the dishes together, and as I was hanging up the dishtowel to dry she moved closer to me and laid her head on my shoulder. I gathered her into my arms and kissed her, softly at first and then more intensely. Wordlessly, I took her into the small guest bedroom and we proceeded to make love together. Our evenings did not always end this way, although more often than not they did. I won't say that my sometime couplings with Joyce were entirely without emotional involvement, because I liked her. I truly did. Perhaps I even loved her somewhat, but not with that overpowering sort of thing. Maybe I'm more of a romanticist than I realize—the big love comes only once. I think Joyce understood that about me.

We were lying together in the guest bed after we finished, a sheet drawn up around us, and I reached over and found some cigarettes on the bedside table, then lit one for each of us. She smoked hers silently for a few moments and then asked: "Happy, Brian?"

"I am right now, at this moment."

"But not all the other moments?"

"Some of them. Not too many of them, though. Not enough of them, Joyce."

She gazed at me for a moment. "It's been three years now, Brian. It's been long enough. You should think about getting married again. It's a great institution, they say."

There was some irony in her voice, and I smiled at her. I knew that she wasn't making a suggestion that she and I should get married. We both knew, instinctively, that it would never work. But she was concerned about me. A good-hearted kid. Her husband lost a hell of a good thing when he walked out on her. "Maybe. Someday. I'll see, Joyce."

"If you ever do, I'll be there in your rooting section, Brian."

"I hope you'll always be in my rooting section."

We finished our cigarettes, and she asked me what time it was. I found my wrist watch on the bedside table and told her it was eleven fifteen.

"I promised the baby-sitter I'd be home by eleven thirty," she said, pulling the sheet down and getting out of the bed. I lay there, watching her walk briskly toward the bathroom, her firm buttocks bouncing nicely. When I heard the water splashing in the bathroom I rose from the bed and put on my slacks again, and when she was finished I escorted her out to the car, carrying the empty pan for her. She slid behind the wheel and I kissed her lightly on the cheek, saying: "Thanks for the meal. Thanks for everything. You're one of the few good things in my life."

She smiled softly. "I'm glad."

When her car had driven away, I returned to the house and poured myself a glass of Scotch, placing a piece of cut lime in it. I was moving out toward the pool area again when the phone rang. It was Tom Ferris.

"Did I interrupt anything?" he asked laconically.

"Not now," I said. "I had a troop of boy scouts in here all evening, and I was teaching them how to tie knots. But the troop just left."

"I'll bet. I wanted to clue you in on the program tomorrow for the reception of your friend Georges Hervé."

"Shoot," I said, cradling the phone against my chin while I stirred the piece of lime in my drink.

"I'm going to put four operatives on the job at first. I'll have one up at the Air France gate, and he can spread a little bread around the airline personnel to get some help in picking this guy up right away. He'll be our lead spotter. The second man I'll have out in front, moving ahead of the subject. And then I'll have two operatives in a car outside, waiting to pick him up as he comes out, and they'll stay right with him."

"Sounds like a good umbrella."

"You're getting an A-l job on this."

"That's why I like your little organization."

"Do you want periodic reports on the Frenchman's activities?"

"Yeah, you'd better keep me clued in regularly during the time he's here. Keep checking in with my office. If I'm not there, I'll get the message from Annie or the answering service."

"Will do. You'll get your first report after we pick up the subject at the airport tomorrow."

I hung up the phone, then wandered out to the pool area and settled down in one of the chairs Joyce and I had occupied a few hours earlier. Tom Ferris seemed to have the whole situation pretty well in control. But, still, I couldn't work up much interest or enthusiasm for this case.

I finished my drink, returned to the bar for another, and then went out to the poolside again. Maybe I should take a trip for myself. Get out the cabin cruiser and sail along some of the inland waterways, or perhaps take it out into the ocean a bit and float along the coastline. But even that didn't seem very appetizing. What I needed—well, what I needed, of course, was Marge. But it was ridiculous and dangerous to allow myself to start thinking like that again.

Perhaps I should sell this house, or more properly, retire the mortgage and buy something else. I had thought of doing that at first and maybe I should have, but when the senator brought me back from Florida the place was still there, and it seemed more simple just to move right back in. And I imagine that was another evidence of my latent romanticism, too—that was the house in which Marge and I had those good years together.

I had first met Marge at one of those parties to which they are always inviting military officers in Washington. She was a petite brunette, the daughter of a U.S. senator from the Midwest. The senator had been in Congress for almost thirty years, and his daughter had been born and reared in the Washington area. I was assigned to the Pentagon at that time and finishing out the last part of my hitch with Army Intelligence. I had spent three years at it—two of them abroad, both in London and Paris—and I was itching then to get back to California and see if I could do anything with that football business. I had played guard position at UCLA, although I was a back in high school. But, since they had a history of light lines in California, they switched me to the line even though I was only about 210 or 215, reasonably heavy for a California lineman. That wasn't big enough for the pros, of course, and I wasn't drafted by any of the teams. But I did apply to the Rams as a free agent, requesting to try out for the backfield. I wasn't doing too badly in training camp, and I might have made the team, or the taxi squad at least, but in a scrimmage on one of those hot July days when I wasn't wearing full pads I got hit high and low while I was turning the end on a sweep-around, and I could almost hear the ligament tear in my knee. End of football for that year.

I was drafted a few months later and nursed the knee back into shape and continued to work out, and I wanted to go back and try it again. But, of course, I never did. Marge and I were married three months after we met, and she tamed me. I settled down in the Washington area, and the senator directed me into a public relations-lobby job. He said the football and army background would help, and I guess it did. I got along reasonably well, a domesticated and contented animal. We purchased the house in Virginia, and shortly after we moved in Marge had our first child, a daughter whom we christened Debbie. It was an almost idyllic existence, and I was amazed at myself that I had settled down so easily.

Three years ago. That was the bad year. First of all, the senator was unexpectedly defeated for re-election, despite the Gallup poll and all the predictions. Some young firebrand in his early thirties mounted a campaign against him, charging that the senator was too old and that new blood was needed in Congress. Two errors in that: first, the senator was not too old, and in fact was still one of the most accomplished practitioners in the Senate; second, although new blood was desirable in Congress, it was not the new blood of the young firebrand who as yet still has to show me that he can achieve anything in the labyrinth ways of the U.S. Congress. But the senator took his defeat gracefully, and prepared to return to his home state where he promised to catch up on his fishing and hunting. In fact, I was in the senator's office that terrible afternoon, helping him tie up some loose ends in Washington, when the phone call came: Marge had been in an automobile accident. She had been driving Debbie to the doctor for a checkup when somebody had ploughed into them, and they were both in the emergency room of Faquier Hospital in Virginia. And in very serious condition.

We drove over in my car, careening through the traffic at the highest speed I could reasonably negotiate. The emergency room seemed filled with policemen when we arrived, and I can remember shouting, "Where is she, where is she?" A doctor in a green scrub-suit had me by the arm, and he kept pulling me aside until he finally got me seated down on a bench and told me softly that she had just died on the table in the back room. Debbie had died immediately in the crash, but they didn't tell us that on the phone.

I'm still not clear about what happened in the next half-hour. I remember them telling me that two teen-age boys in some kind of hot rod had lost control of their car, crossed the middle lane, and slammed into Marge head-on. I must have still been sitting on the bench when they brought one of the boys out of the back room, only a small strip of adhesive plaster over one eye. They tell me I sprung up and went for the kid. I managed to get one hand on the kid's shoulder, and I was measuring him when a cop grabbed me from behind. I whirled and flattened the cop with a karate chop across the neck, and reached for the kid again, who was now cowering away from me in a corner. I got him around the throat this time and was squeezing him quickly with that rapid technique I had learned in Army Intelligence. They told me that one of the other cops had to let me have it across the back of the head with a club, one sharp blow that knocked me out.

They carried me into the back room and brought me around, and when I finally regained consciousness I can remember the senator standing over me, his eyes dull with pain and concern. Nobody pressed any charges against me, the distraught new widower. But it didn't make any difference, anyway. Everything was over for me, as far as I was concerned. I went through the motions of the funeral with surprising control, looking at those two coffins, the large one and the small white one. But when it was over I fell apart completely, just sitting around the house and lapping up the booze.

I guess it was two weeks later that the insurance man came and presented me with the check for fifty thousand dollars, the result of the little policy Marge and I had taken out on each other to help take care of Debbie in case anything should happen to either of us. I kept looking at the check for a couple of days, and a few times I almost tore it up. But eventually I deposited it in my checking account. Maybe I could use some of it to get myself straightened out. I took a plane down to Florida and ended up in the Keys. I tried to do some fishing and some sailing, but nothing seemed to work.

I had rented a house near the beach, and before too long I established a distressing pattern for myself: Drag myself out of bed late in the morning, bring myself around with some Bloody Mary's, lay on the beach for awhile—perhaps with a screwdriver or two in my hand—and then, of course, the long series of Gibsons before dinner in some restaurant, and then the Scotches into the dark night. I made a few friends, picked up some girls once in awhile, but even that didn't do any good. In fact, it made me feel immeasurably worse.

Six months later I was 240 pounds, and well on the way to becoming the champion beach-bum of the Keys. Somehow the senator found me, and one morning when I woke up he was sitting there beside the bed. He told me that he had come to take me back to Washington. I don't know how he talked me into it, because I didn't want to go. Maybe my brain was so fogged with alcohol that I couldn't think of reasoned arguments against him; but somehow he got me out of there and back to D.C.

And then … well, you know the rest of the lousy story.

I had finished my drink and now I picked the lime from the bottom of the empty glass and sucked on it for awhile. Finally, I threw it away, peeled off my clothes, and dove into the pool naked. I did four laps and when I pulled myself up on the edge of the pool, dripping with water, I felt tired enough to go to sleep.

CHAPTER THREE

I had lunch with Senator Henry Phillips in the Senate dining room the next day.

It was a long, leisurely lunch, but we only had to spend a few minutes talking about the strip-mining situation in West Virginia. Most of the time Hank reminisced about the old days, particularly when the old senator was still in town. Therefore, it was almost three thirty when I reached my office, and Annie had already departed for the day. I decided to sit around for awhile and see if Tom Ferris would call to give me an initial report on the arrival of the Air France from Paris.

He did, and it was a disturbing report.

The call came about four thirty, and there was disgust in Tom's voice. "A foul-up," he said.

"You lost him?"

"I don't lose people, Brian. Your Georges Hervé wasn't on that flight."

"Are you sure?"

"Of course, I'm sure," he said impatiently.

"No chance he could have slipped by your men?"

"Not a chance in the world. My boys did a nice job. They even made a deal with the guy who rides those little passenger buses out to the airplanes. This guy was to get a look at the passenger manifest from one of the hostesses and point out Hervé, but the hostess said that there was nobody on the plane by that name. So my boys scrutinized everybody who came out of those doors.

The plane was only about a third full, and it was easy. But there was nobody faintly resembling the description of the subject you described to me."

"Any chance of a disguise?"

"I had good men out there. They can spot a disguise a football field away."

"Oh, hell," I said.

"I'm not through on this yet," Tom said. "I'm having Air France check this out through their teletype reservation system. I want to know if Hervé even had a reservation on this flight. Maybe he got waylaid in Paris before he got on board."

"That's a great thought," I said.

"Stay in your office for a little while, will you? I should have some dope on this in a short while, and I'll call you back."

I lighted a cigarette while waiting for Ferris to call me back, and thought: "Oh, damn, a simple little job like this and it gets botched up. Maybe the whole deal is off, anyway; maybe this Hervé cancelled out his trip." That would mean that I'd have to get Annie to fish the ten thou out of the bank and return it to the French Embassy. I considered for a moment phoning the embassy and asking them what was up. I could talk to that Ballard woman, or even to Duval. But I dismissed that idea immediately. They didn't want me checking in there, and if they wanted their money back they'd sure as hell call *me*.

Ferris phoned me twenty minutes later. "I've got something," he said. "There was no Hervé on the passenger manifest in Paris. But, get this. A Georges Hervé was originally scheduled to make the flight, but a few hours before flight time he cancelled out and made a reservation on the exact same flight for tomorrow. Is that your man?"

"I don't know. It sounds like him."

"You could make my job a little easier, Brian, if you could tell me what this change of reservations is all about."

"I'll be damned if I know, Tom."

"Well, do you want me to set up the same umbrella for the Air France flight tomorrow?"

"I guess so," I said uncertainly.

"Don't sound so enthusiastic about it."

"I'm sorry, Tom. Yes, by all means set up the umbrella again. And maybe in the meantime I can make some sense out of this."

I sat at my desk for a little while longer, trying to sort it out in my mind. The Georges Hervé of tomorrow's flight was undoubtedly the same one who was due today. But I sure as hell wish the embassy had let me know about the change of plans. However, maybe the embassy wasn't even aware of it. People do change plans at the last moment. Of course, there was always the remote possibility that tomorrow's Hervé was not the same man, but that sounded implausible. Of even greater possibility, I reasoned, was the chance that that Hervé would cancel out again tomorrow. Maybe the deal he had been working on, whatever it was, had fallen through and he had merely made another reservation on the slim possibility that things would clear up. Round and round. I stopped myself. What the hell do I care if he ever comes over here? If the trip cancels out, I'll still bill the embassy for Tom's work and a healthy stipend for my time. I'll return part of the ten thousand, but I'll keep a good slice of it.

I rose and was about to leave the office when the phone rang again.

"Monsieur Petersen," the voice said. It was the Ballard woman from the embassy.

"Oh, yes, Mademoiselle Ballard. How are you?" I was going to let her do the talking.

"There has been a regrettable change in Monsieur Hervé's travel plans."

"Yes?" I said guardedly.

"Monsieur Hervé did not arrive today. But, of course, you must know this."

"Yes, I know it. We had four operatives out at Dulles, and all they did was waste their time."

"I am so sorry. We received word only at the very last moment. And there was no opportunity to get in contact with you before the plane arrived."

For some reason I doubted that. Maybe they decided to let me go through with the reception so they could see, in some sort of dry run, how good a job I would do. Well, I do a damned good job, and if that's what they were doing, they could take this job and forget it. But maybe I was being unfair to them. I reeled myself in and said: "Is the assignment still on, Mademoiselle Ballard?"

"Oh, yes. Yes, indeed."

"And the Georges Hervé who is scheduled to arrive on the afternoon flight tomorrow is the same man?"

"Ah, you know about that already."

I felt an irrational smugness and merely grunted, "Yes."

"Excellent," she said. "Monsieur Duval was right about you. You are very thorough. Yes, please, the very exact same arrangements."

"I hope he makes tomorrow's flight."

She must have sensed some annoyance in my voice, because she very quickly said, "I am sure he will. I am so sorry for this little ... inconvenience."

"All right, Mademoiselle Ballard," I said, but as I hung up the phone I decided for myself that if Hervé wasn't on tomorrow's plane I was going to pull off the assignment and the embassy could get somebody else. That was a childish reaction, I know, but it was part of the mood I was in.

However, the Frenchman did arrive the next day, exactly as scheduled. The plane was on time, and Tom Ferris phoned me at my office immediately after he received the first report from one of his operatives. I had been waiting in the office for either Ferris or the Ballard woman to phone me. And if Hervé had not been on that plane, then I was going to cancel the whole thing.

"An easy mark," Tom was telling me on the phone. "Your Frenchman was a simple target. My boys fixed up the same deal as yesterday, and the gateman pointed out Hervé to us. But even that really wasn't necessary. You couldn't miss him. Just as you described him. Short Frenchy with a mustache. Homburg, dark clothes, the works."

"Where is he now?"

"On his way into town. I've got a car following him with two men in it. And I've got another man waiting down at the Mayflower for him to arrive. We've phoned ahead the license number of Hervé's taxi, and my man at the Mayflower will pick him up as he arrives. He can get right behind Hervé as he checks in, find out his room number, and get a room on the same floor right near him. Then we can set up a watch station right there."

"Smooth, Tom." I could relax now: Ferris had the situation well in hand; he was doing the professional job for which he was noted.

And so it went, on and on, as I permitted myself to get deeper into it, allowing myself to be lulled into an even more dangerous complacency.

Later that evening, Tom called me at home to report that the protective network he had set up was working quite efficiently.

The Frenchman had a room on the sixth floor at the Mayflower, and one of Tom's operatives had managed to obtain a room almost directly across the corridor from him, while another operative was downstairs in the lobby waiting to pick him up if he should come down.

"I think I can even do this with two men now," Tom told me over the phone. "Apparently he's not going to move around too much. A quiet little guy. Had some supper sent up to his room. And about a half-hour ago he went downstairs and took a short stroll along Connecticut Avenue for a few blocks, puffing a cigarette. About ten minutes, and he went right back to his room. I think he's in for the night now."

"Has he had any visitors?"

"None at all. And he's only registered to stay for two nights."

"That's good. Now, just let's get him out of town without any bruises, and we've earned our money."

I was feeling so complacent about Tom's expert handling of the situation that I rode out to Burning Tree late the next morning and shot nine fast holes of golf.

But when I reached the office about two o'clock Annie told me that both Ferris and Therese Ballard had called, the latter three different times.

"I told her I didn't know when you'd be back," Annie said, 'but she wouldn't leave any number where you could reach her. She said she'd just keep calling."

"No, she wouldn't leave a number," I said. "She's supposed to contact me."

A smile of triumph came over Annie's face. "Ah, but the last time she called I got a number out of her. I told her that she might not be able to contact you today at all, since you'd be in and out of the office, and if she really wanted you she'd better leave word for you to call her." Annie handed me a slip of paper with a phone number written on it. "Call her there as soon as you can."

I took the slip of paper into my office and lay it on my desk. But first I called Ferris. He had nothing exciting to report. The Frenchman had not even left the hotel today; he ate both breakfast and lunch in his room. But Tom's operative had learned, by throwing a few dollars to the telephone operator, that Hervé had ordered a chauffeured car for the evening, which he wanted to have take him out to someplace in Chevy Chase. Tom's men, of course, would follow right along.

I dialed the number Annie had given me, and Therese Ballard answered it on the first ring. "Oh, Monsieur Petersen. Thank you for calling. I have to speak to you today."

"Everything's going fine with your Mr. Hervé," I told her, and I gave her a summary of what Ferris had reported. "This is his last night in town," I said, "and these private operatives will follow him closely during his trip to Chevy Chase."

"Ah, yes," she said slowly over the phone, and then paused. "There is, Monsieur Petersen, a little … complication …"

It seemed too easy, I told myself, and said: "Yes?"

"We have received notice from Paris that news of Monsieur Hervé's trip has become known, and we are afraid now that he might very well be disturbed by representatives of rival firms who are interested in what he's doing."

"You only asked me to insure his safety. I can't manage whom he talks to."

"Yes," she said, musingly. "Tell me, Mr. Petersen. This detective firm you have employed, it is a good one?"

"The very best."

Again, there was a pause before she said: "I am going to ask you a great favor, Mr. Petersen. This meeting tonight is the heart of Monsieur Hervé's trip. Would you, personally, escort him to where he is going?"

"Mademoiselle Ballard, I'm no escort. The detectives will do a much better job of protecting him than I can."

"I have discussed this with the ambassador, and we feel that since news of Monsieur Hervé's trip is known, there is no harm now in letting him know that the embassy is watching out for his interests. If you would go to the hotel, present yourself to Monsieur Hervé, and then escort him tonight, we would all feel much at ease about it."

"I'm not a private bodyguard," I said sharply.

"Oh, we realize that, Monsieur Petersen. But we have so much confidence in you. We would be so grateful...." her voice trailed off.

It was the hand-on-the-arm routine again, except that I couldn't smell the perfume this time. I was about to make an emphatic refusal, when I said to myself; What the hell! I didn't have anything special planned for that night. I thought that perhaps I might go back to Burning Tree again later in the afternoon and see if I could keep that golf score under eighty. But that would still mean another nothing night at the empty house in Virginia. Furthermore, I was getting tired of working out this assignment on the phone. Restless, I guess. Maybe a little something different would snap me out of it. "Okay, Mademoiselle Ballard," I said finally.

"We are most grateful, Monsieur Petersen. And we will have to think about some further reimbursement for your added efforts."

"We'll see," I said.

I phoned Ferris and told him that I was going to take over as the escort for Hervé this evening. He didn't seem very happy about that, but when I cut him off sharply, he told me he'd meet me in the lobby of the Mayflower at five thirty to point out his operatives to me so that they could arrange the pass-over of the subject.

The lobby of the Mayflower was crowded when I arrived, and there were long lines of people at the registration desk. It was check-in time for the people who were arriving for tomorrow's business. The lobby of the hotel had been completely redecorated a few years ago, and it was now all bright and fresh in gleaming gilds and pastels. But I rather liked it better the old way because it somehow characterized, despite its slight dowdiness, the nature of the institution: a dignified and venerable hotel only a short distance from the White House. I saw Tom standing on the far side of the lobby near the assistant manager's desk and thumbing casually through the *Evening Star.* Tom is a large man, about six feet, with a protruding stomach now grown out of control and a florid complexion. He seems to always wear a slight frown, as if he were either trying to figure out some problem or perhaps had eaten something that hadn't quite agreed with him. He was in his early fifties, but his hair was still surprisingly good, full and reddish with flecks of gray throughout. Standing there in the lobby, he could have been a salesman, or an insurance agent, or an accountant—anything but a private detective.

He saw me immediately, folded his paper, and walked slowly toward me. He still didn't look happy. "You got a license to work as an operative?" he asked, only a faint trace of humor in his voice.

"Sorry, Tom. Client's orders."

"I'd tell the client to stick it." I shrugged my shoulders, and he persisted: "One of my men can tag after you, anyway." He nodded his head at the large circular couch in the middle of the lobby where a conservatively dressed man in his early forties was sitting. One of Tom's operatives. He had a briefcase resting on the seat next to him, and he appeared to be someone waiting for a business appointment.

"That won't be necessary. Besides," I smiled, "I can save myself some money that way."

"The hell with the money. I won't charge you any extra."

"It's okay. I can manage. Keep the fellow in the room upstairs, and when we get back he can pick up the trail again. Also, we're bringing this out in the open tonight, so I can ask Hervé his plans for tomorrow, and you'll only need one man."

Tom still didn't appear pleased. "Do you want a weapon for tonight?" he asked.

"I've got one," I said. Before I left the office I had taken my Smith and Wesson .32 out of the office safe. It's a little gun, I realized, weighing only eighteen ounces and holding six shells, but it suited my purposes. You could carry it easily, and sometimes I could almost palm it in my hand. I didn't like to use the gun unless I really had to, and at short range you can pump a .32 slug just as well as any other. And furthermore, whenever you had to pull a gun on somebody to quiet them down, the .32 looked just as menacing as a large German Luger. This evening I was wearing the revolver in a thin holster hitched to the rear of my belt under the jacket of my suit.

"I'll call Hervé on the house phone," I said to Walsh. "What's his room number?"

"634."

I used one of the house phones on the ledge near the cashier's desk, gave the operator the number, but had to wait quite awhile before it answered.

"*Allo,*" the man's voice said in a thick French accent.

"Monsieur Hervé, my name is Brian Petersen, and the French Embassy asked me to contact you...."

"The French Embassy," he repeated. "I don't want to speak to anybody from the embassy. Nobody at all. Please leave me alone." And he hung up abruptly.

"Great," I thought. I went over and told Tom about it, and he almost laughed.

"What system do your men have for picking him up when he comes down?" I asked Tom.

"The operative in the room has his door on a crack, and when Hervé leaves, he phones the desk clerk and asks him to tell Mr. Smith, or whatever name we're using, that he'll be right down. Then the upstairs operative follows him down on the elevator, and in the meantime our Mr. Smith sitting over there, who has already identified himself to the desk clerk, has received word that his party is coming down to meet him So we've got the web set up before the subject reaches the lobby floor—one man in front, one behind."

"Tell your man to let me know when Hervé is coming down and point him out to me."

Tom walked over toward the newspaper stand and somehow must have signaled his operative, because a few seconds later he rose and joined Tom near the stand. Tom returned to me, and the operative resumed his seat on the couch.

"I want to stay here and watch this," Tom said, a smirk on his face.

We had to wait almost a half-hour before the operative rose and went over to the desk clerk. He said something, smiled at him, and began to wander over to the elevator door. A minute later one of the doors opened, and about half a dozen people moved out. I watched the eye exchange between Tom and his operative. The operative looked over at Tom meaningfully, and then back at a small man in a dark-blue suit. Mustache, homburg in one hand, briefcase in the other. Tom started to say something to me, but I interrupted him: "I got it. I'll see you."

I intercepted Hervé as he approached the middle of the lobby, on his way toward the Connecticut Avenue entrance. "Monsieur Hervé," I said, handing him one of my business cards.

He paused, looked at the card, but refused to take it. "*Excusez-moi*, I am in very much of a hurry." He tried to brush past me.

"This will only take a minute. The French Embassy asked me to contact you."

He looked puzzled for a moment. "The phone. You were the man on the phone."

"Yes."

"I told you I do not want to have any business with the embassy." He searched my face as if he was trying to recall where he had seen it before. "Have I met you?" he asked.

"No sir. I am just working with the embassy on this one assignment."

"Assignment?"

"The embassy would like to assure your comfort and safety while you are in Washington, and they asked me to accompany you to your appointment in Chevy Chase this evening."

"My appointment in Chevy Chase," he repeated incredulously. "Ah, yes, I imagine the embassy would know something about that."

I didn't dare tell him how I had obtained that information, because it might make him even more distrustful of me. "I'd be very happy to drive you out there in my car, sir, wait for you, and bring you back."

He studied my face for a few moments, trying to ascertain if he could trust me. Finally, he reached out and took my business card, studied it carefully. "*Bon*," he said, nodding his head. "That is very kind of you, Mr. Petersen. I accept your offer." He placed my card in his pocket.

We left the hotel together through the Connecticut Avenue entrance, and as we neared the door I observed Tom Ferris watching us over the edge of the paper he was reading. I winked slyly at him.

CHAPTER FOUR

After my initial difficulties with Georges Hervé, he seemed to relax and was quite cordial with me.

In front of the hotel I told the doorman to cancel the car Hervé had ordered, and I escorted the Frenchman to my Oldsmobile, which was parked a few steps from the main door. When I opened the door for him, he said: "*Merci beaucoup. Vous êtes très gentil.*"

We drove leisurely straight out Connecticut Avenue toward Chevy Chase, and I tried some of my French on him. My French was never very good, but even that was exceedingly rusty now. Hervé, however, was polite about it, trying to listen attentively and then answer carefully and deliberately in a measured French I could not fail to understand. I attempted to point out some of the sights along the way—the hotels, Rock Creek Park, the tree-lined avenue, the private homes. But finally my labored French gave out, and I lapsed into silence. I reached over toward the radio dial and asked: "Music?"

"*Ah, le radio. Oui.*"

I found one of those stations that plays soft dinner music, and as we drove along in silence, Hervé lit a cigarette and scanned the passing scene through my closed windows. The air-conditioning was working nicely.

The address he gave me was only a few blocks from Chevy Chase Circle, and I spun around the circle and then off into the quieter residential section of bigger homes. I found the street fairly easily, slowed down, and began searching for house numbers. Hervé had never been here before, and so he was no help. The numbers were hard to read, some of them tacked on obscure little signs situated at odd places on the front lawn, others covered by vines, and some removed completely. Finally, we found it, a stately brick house situated on a kind of small hill with a large sloping lawn that ran down to the sidewalk. Two other cars were parked directly in front of the house, and so I parked behind them, only a few yards from the pathway. As I was parking, another car, a four-door sedan, pulled into the curb about fifty yards behind me. Through the rear-view mirror I could see that it contained only one person, a man.

Hervé asked me if I wanted to join him and wait inside while he completed his business. The house belonged to a French lawyer, he told me, and he thought his negotiations would only take a few minutes. I demurred, but when he insisted, telling me it would be cooler and more comfortable inside, I finally agreed. We both alighted from the car at the same time, and I walked around to join him on the sidewalk. It was still light, and the heat of the day had not dissipated one bit.

We were walking along the sidewalk, almost at the pathway up to the house, when I heard the sound behind me. Not a heavy sound, but a very soft and gentle thump. I guess my ears are more attuned to such odd and slight noises than most people, because Hervé did not seem to hear it. I glanced quickly over my shoulder, and I saw it.

In fact, I saw the whole thing in one glance—four men coming at us, stocking masks over their faces, two of them with knives in their hands. And the other fellow still sitting in the car, the doors now open.

It's amazing how quickly your mind can work in such situations. I realized that these four men had been crouched in the car, which had followed us for God knows how long. More carelessness on my part, because I had not taken the simple precautions to spot or lose a tail. That damned lethargic mood I had been in. Well—I was suddenly out of it now.

When I spun around, the two lead attackers picked up speed, rushing at us, their knives extended. I noticed, curiously, that they were wearing some kind of felt soles on their shoes that cut down on the sound. I shouted at Hervé, and he wheeled, standing there frozen. One man was making for me, the other for Hervé. In the split seconds before they reached us, I tried to act in exactly the same manner as Hervé—terrified, immobilized, slightly cowering. And then, just as they were about to hit us, I reached over and gave Hervé a terrific shove that sent him sprawling on the grassy strip next to the sidewalk. I completed the motion by lunging at the man who was charging at me with the knife.

The basic principle of judo is to use the motion of the attacker against himself. I wasn't a pure judo man, because I had devised a little private combination of judo and karate, but this motion was principally judo. My attacker was surprised that I had come to life, but by that time it was too late. I had grabbed him someplace around the upper forearm, and using the acceleration of his charge, I kept him going, up in the air, bumping him roughly with my shoulder as he went over. I didn't stop to look where he fell, but I heard him groan as he hit the ground. The other attacker had changed his course and landed right on the top of Hervé, but I couldn't see whether or not he had been able to get the knife into him. He was now kneeling over him, about to go through his pockets; and, of course, the other two guys were coming up quickly on me. It had to be fast again. I reached behind my belt, getting the .32 out in one swoop, and at the same time I aimed a kick at the fellow bending over Hervé, catching him right in the stomach and sending him sprawling.

Then I turned to the other two attackers. They had cleverly split, so that they were coming at me from different angles. And, for the first time, I noticed that they were all dressed pretty much the same way—dark trousers, a kind of sweatshirt that came down to their wrists, and the stocking masks over their faces. The only part of their flesh that was exposed was their hands, and they were black.

I fired directly into the chest of the one coming from my left. One leg went out from under him immediately, and he went down. I was whirling to fire at the one coming from my right when he dove at me. It was a beautiful hit. His hand crashed across my wrist, knocking the revolver out of my hand, and at the same time his knee got me in the stomach, hard and fast. It was a professional movement, and I knew then that these guys were pros and I was in deep trouble.

I went down on one knee under the impact, gasping for breath, and he let me have it again. A karate chop aimed for the neck. However, I saw it coming and I managed to roll away from it a bit, so that it caught me on the shoulder. I went all the way down then, and out of the corner of my eye I saw that the one I had kicked was back on top of Hervé again. I tried to roll away but my assailant fell right on top of me, letting me have another knee in the stomach. I heaved upward, pushing him off and rolling him over on the ground. I had to get back to Hervé and be careful of the first man who had attacked me, the one I sent spinning into the air. I wasn't sure whether he was unconscious or not.

He wasn't, as I realized later, because just then I was cracked from behind. It was a perfectly aimed chop across the back of my neck, and it finished me off. I went out flat on the ground, not completely unconscious, but totally incapable of movement.

I heard some voices, some shuffling of feet, and then a car pull away, its motor roaring furiously. There was silence for a moment, then more voices. A woman screaming. Someone shouting, "Call the police!"

I tried to pull myself up, painfully, but I fell back again. Another effort and I was up on one elbow, attempting to focus my eyes. There was a sharp pain in my left shoulder, and I realized that one of them had finally gotten his knife into me, probably after I went out. Blood was streaming down the front of my shirt.

I looked around for Hervé, and I saw him lying in the same spot where he had originally been attacked. One look was all I needed—he was dead.

I sat up, and with my right hand I pounded the pavement once in fierce anger. More than anger. Rage. Fury. I was quite sure at that moment that I knew the whole story, although I was going to check it out with infinite care. You're damn right I was going to check it out, because I was certain that I had been played for the perfect patsy.

Therese Ballard had made me her pigeon.

The police arrived with amazing rapidity—first a single squad car, and then four or five more. By the time the first one arrived I was sitting up, supported by someone from one of the houses on the street, a young man in his middle twenties who kept telling me to take it easy. Somebody else was bending over Hervé, attempting to see what could be done for him, but I growled, "Leave him alone, he's dead." They had done a pretty good job on Hervé—a slash across the throat and a number of knife pumps in his chest. I could see that two of his pockets were turned inside out, and they had probably lifted everything from him. His briefcase, of course, was gone.

I ripped open my shirt, tearing it gently away from me to inspect my own wound. It wasn't very deep, just a slash of four or five inches right on my shoulder, but it was bleeding quite freely. I wadded up a piece of my torn shirt and pressed it against the wound to halt the flow of the blood. As I began to get my perspective, I noticed that my own wallet, which I carried in my inner coat pocket, was gone. And something else—despite the blood all over my suit jacket, I was able to observe a large smear of black substance across the middle of the jacket, something like black coal grease.

I knew what that black stain was.

A policeman was asking me how I was, and I told him that it was just a surface wound. He then asked me my name, which I told him, and then the name of the other man.

"Georges Hervé, a Frenchman."

"A diplomat?" the policeman asked, anxiety in his voice.

"No, just a visiting businessman." The cop seemed relatively relieved at that. An attack on a member of the diplomatic corps was a much more serious episode.

"What happened?" the policeman asked. He had a notebook and was writing down my answers.

I could tell him a lot, but I thought I'd just give him the obvious facts. "I had parked my car and was walking toward the house there," I said, nodding my head toward the brick house. A large number of people were standing around now, looking at the macabre scene and being held back from it by other policemen. I wondered which of them was the one Hervé had been on his way to see. "We were walking along the sidewalk when we got jumped from behind by four footpads. A little struggle, and you can see what happened."

"Descriptions?" the policeman asked tersely.

"No help," I said shaking my head. "They were all wearing those silk stockings pulled down over their faces and right down to the neckbands of their sweatshirts. All of them were of average build, but they were fast and they were good."

The policeman, a young fellow still in his twenties, nodded understandingly, as if this were something he encountered every day, and he wrote some more in his notebook. I had been still sitting on the ground, and now I laboriously pulled myself to my feet. The policeman pointed to another pool of blood, some ten feet away from where I had been sitting. "Know what that is?" he asked.

I nodded my head. "I got one of them with my .32 before it was knocked out of my hand."

"That's your weapon, then?" he asked and pointed to another policeman who was standing over near Hervé's body. The policeman had inserted a pencil into the barrel of the gun so that he wouldn't rub his own fingerprints on it, and now he was inspecting it carefully.

"Yeah," I said. "May I have it back now?"

"We'll have to keep it for awhile. Check it out. Do you have a permit?"

"Yes," I said wearily, "I have a permit. For protection. So I can protect myself against things like this," and I waved toward Hervé's body.

"Yeah," the policeman agreed. "Theft and violence on the streets—they're getting out of control."

I nodded my head. The policeman had it all wrapped up—another mugging in a violent society. But, of course, I knew it was much more than a straight mugging.

An ambulance arrived, a volunteer rescue service that came to the aid of people in this affluent suburb, and one of the drivers walked over to me immediately, a first-aid kit in his hand. "Is the bleeding stopped?" he asked me.

"No, it has to be sewn up. Give me some of those gauze squares from your kit."

I slipped off my jacket, which was still hanging on my right arm, and it fell to the ground. I noted ruefully that my Hickey-Freeman suit was ruined, a slash in the jacket and a long tear up the trouser leg. Another score, although a minor one, to be settled with Miss Ballard and her friends.

There was some discussion a few feet away between the policemen and the ambulance driver whether or not to put Hervé in the ambulance with me. The driver was protesting that the man was dead, and one of the cops was saying that you couldn't be sure. But just then an unmarked car arrived with some plain-clothesmen, and they took control of the situation. Hervé was going to stay there for awhile, until the butcher wagon came and took him to the morgue.

I climbed into the rear door of the ambulance, then sat on the stretcher and took one last look at Georges Hervé. His mouth was open, and there was a strange expression on his face—not so much pain as surprise and bewilderment. I had met him less than an hour ago; he had seemed like a harmless little fellow, slightly nervous but polite and deferential. And now he was lying dead on a sidewalk in suburban Washington.

One of the plain-clothesmen bent over Hervée's body, and with a piece of chalk began to outline the position of the prone body. The ambulance started up, its siren blaring, a red light blinking brightly on the top of it, and we drove away.

I sat on the stretcher for a few minutes, but then I decided to lie down, pressing the blood-matted gauze against the wound in my shoulder. The siren blared loudly—too loudly, I thought.

We pulled in at the emergency-room door of the Washington Hospital Center, and despite the driver's protests, I walked in through the swinging doors. There were only two people sitting in the waiting area—an old man who held a rag against his forehead, pressing it on some bump he had received, and a fat woman in a housecoat who was sitting there with a strained expression on her face. The ambulance driver went over to the nurse and began whispering something to her, nodding once in my direction. She came over immediately and asked to look at my wound. I pried the gauze away from it, and she examined it carefully. It didn't look too bad now—the bleeding had abated considerably. But nevertheless it was gaping, and it required some sutures to hold it together. She told me to sit down, and the doctor would be there in a few minutes.

But instead of sitting down, I followed her into her little glass-paneled office. "I want to use your phone," I said.

"That phone isn't for private calls. Only for hospital business," she said, frowning.

I already had my hand on the receiver. "Don't worry about it," I told her as I picked it up. She appeared ready to protest again, but then she whirled and walked away toward someplace in one of the back rooms.

I phoned Tom Ferris at his home. One of the teen-age children answered, and I asked for his father.

"Trouble?" Tom asked when he came on the line.

"More than I could handle. We got jumped by four guys on a sidewalk in Chevy Chase. Hervé is dead, and I've got a minor knife wound."

"Jesus! Where are you?"

"Washington Hospital Center."

"I'll be right there."

"Before you leave, get something arranged for me. I want one of those artists who construct a picture of somebody from a verbal description."

"I know a few good ones. In fact, one of them works for the police."

"That's the one I want. Have him at my office in, say, forty-five minutes to an hour."

"I don't know if I can get him at this time of night."

I looked at my watch, and for the first time realized that they had slipped my watch from me, too. Damn. The clock on the wall said seven forty. "Just get him there, Tom."

Next I dialed Annie at her home. I didn't tell her what had happened, but I asked her if she could get down to my office in about an hour. An emergency. She agreed. I had one more call to make, but I couldn't remember the number. I dialed Information and asked for the number of the French Embassy. When I had it, I phoned the embassy and some woman answered, probably a maid. I asked her if Monsieur Duval had left the embassy yet. He was married and lived in a small house not too far from the embassy. She told me that he had departed, and I then asked her to get me his home phone number. She mumbled something about the fact that she was not part of the office staff and did not have access to the home phone numbers of the embassy personnel. But I insisted, this time in my fractured French, and she finally agreed to obtain it for me.

I was dialing Duval's home number when the doctor arrived. He wanted me to come right back into the examination room, but I told him I had to make this one call first. He protested, and I said to him: "I've got to call my insurance agent to make sure I have enough coverage to pay for this high-class treatment."

He didn't like that, not at all. But, to his credit, he pulled away the gauze from my wound while I was making the call and looked at it intently.

Duval registered surprise at hearing from me. "I've got to see you right away," I said, and I told him where I was.

"Impossible," he told me. "The ambassador has just phoned me. I have to attend a critically important emergency meeting at the embassy."

"I can tell you what that meeting is going to be about—the death of Georges Hervé."

"*Alors,* you know that?"

"I was there when he was killed. I think it would be worth your while to stop here on the way to the embassy. I want to ask you something, and I can give you some details about Hervé's murder which the ambassador will find very interesting. It's a fair exchange."

"*Bien.* I'll see you very shortly."

"*Immédiatement.*"

"*Oui.*"

I already knew the answer to the big question I was going to ask Duval, but I still wanted to hear it directly from him.

"Okay," I said to the doctor. "Sew me up. A nice cross-stitch." He scowled at me.

CHAPTER FIVE

They stretched me out on a table in the emergency room while the doctor, now wearing rubber gloves, started to insert the sutures into my knife wound. He first shot some novocaine into the fatty tissue around the edge of the wound, and then proceeded efficiently to his work. He was a man in his early thirties, probably a resident in training, and he worked quickly and efficiently. After he had inserted the first suture, he said: "Get this in a fight?"

"Yeah," I said, "but you should see the other fellow." I closed my eyes as he continued to work.

The door swung open and I looked around, hoping to see Tom Ferris. Instead, it was Walt Comber. I might have expected this.

"Beautiful, Brian, beautiful," he said laconically.

"You'll have to wait outside," the doctor said sharply.

"We'll be through in a few minutes."

"Police," Walt announced flatly.

"Can't it wait?" the doctor asked.

"No," Walt said simply.

The doctor pursed his lips, but continued to sew me up.

"All right, Brian, tell me all about it," Walt said.

"Can't you see I'm in intense pain?" I said, closing my eyes again.

Walt Comber sat down on a white metal chair on the far side of the room. "Christ," he said softly. Walt was an old friend of mine, one of the few I had on the D.C. police force. He was a detective in the homicide division, and we had been involved in a few cases together. But we also worked together frequently in areas outside his own division specialty. He has supplied me with a number of good leads in things I've been working on, and he's been able to open some doors for me in the police department that would have otherwise been barred. In turn, I've done a number of things for him, principally obtaining information from sources that weren't readily available to him. I was aware of the fact that Walt was often uneasy about our relationship and that he didn't always quite trust me, but it had worked satisfactorily to our mutual advantage. I just hope that the day never arrives when Walt discovers me in something blatantly illegal, because I'm sure he'd be forced to book me. He was that kind of an honest guy.

"Didn't you read the report?" I asked Comber.

"I read the sing-song you gave the patrolman," Comber said. He took a massive white handkerchief out of his pocket and began mopping his face with it. He was a large man in his early fifties, with a bulging stomach. If Tom Ferris did not convey the flavor of law-enforcement background, then Walt Comber made up for it completely. He looked policeman, from his rumpled dark suit to his heavy-soled shoes, relics of the days when he pounded the beat as a uniformed officer. "Something doesn't ring true about it," he said.

"A simple case," I said, my eyes still closed. "A mugging on a Washington street."

"Nothing with you in it is ever simple."

The doctor had finished his suturing and was now applying a bandage to the wound, taping it securely in place with large strips of adhesive that he wound over my shoulder. I sat up, and the doctor said, "I want to give you a tetanus shot."

"I had one … four months ago."

"Well—if you had one four months ago…." the doctor said reflectively.

"Sure," Comber said. "He's accident prone."

I thanked the doctor, and he left the room, closing the door behind him. Comber pulled a small notebook from his pocket and began studying it. I was sitting on the edge of the table, and I noticed that the remnants of my coat and shirt were lying on another chair. I went over and quickly folded the shirt into a ball, and put on the bloodied jacket. "How'd you get here so quickly?" I asked Comber.

"Picked it up on the police radio. Homicide in the D.C. area of Chevy Chase. Got there right after the ambulance left. And, lo and behold, who do I hear is one of the victims? My old buddy, Brian Petersen." He said it with some kind of mock disdain.

"One of the *living* victims," I said. "There's a difference."

"Who is—" he paused, consulting his notebook, "Georges Hervé?"

"A visiting French businessman."

"And what were you doing with him in Chevy Chase?"

"One of my services. I was escorting him around Washington, and he was going to have dinner with one of his friends in Chevy Chase, and—*zap* we got mugged."

"You always carry a pistol when you go out to dinner?"

"Violent city. If I had known what was going to happen, I would have dragged a cannon along."

He frowned. "You were going to 3861 Spring Street?" Walt asked. "The home of Alphonse Metivier?" He mispronounced the French name terribly.

"Yes," I lied. I had been so careless about this thing, that I hadn't even asked Hervé the name of the resident of the house to which I was driving him. At that time it was really none of my business, but I should have pried it out of him nevertheless. I made a mental note of it now.

"And how did you first meet this Hervé?"

"The French Embassy contacted me and asked me to give him the royal treatment." I hated to do this to Walt, but since my assailants had gone to such elaborate pains to make it look like a street mugging, I thought I'd take the bait and act as if that were really the case. Furthermore, if it were handled as a regular mugging, there was a good chance there would be little publicity about it in the newspapers, and I didn't want any publicity about it right now. I had work to do, and it was best done quietly.

"The French Embassy," Walt repeated. "Christ, is this another one of those goddam embassy things?"

"I don't think so. Hervé wasn't government or diplomatic. Merely a well-to-do businessman whom the embassy wanted to treat royally."

"I'd hardly consider you royal treatment," Walt said dryly.

"Lots of people would dispute that."

"And where was this Hervé staying in town? There's not a scrap of paper on his body. They picked him clean."

"At the Mayflower."

"I suppose we'll have to contact the embassy. French national killed abroad."

"They already know about it."

"Oh?"

"I called them," I said quickly.

He shook his head slowly. "I still don't think you're giving me all the facts." He eyed me suspiciously.

"Believe me, Walt. I'm giving you all the *facts* I have now. I'm going to do some checking on this myself, and if I come up with anything I'll let you know. I promise you."

He still didn't appear convinced. "I wish you'd cooperate more with the police, Brian."

"Is the interrogation completed, Lieutenant?"

"I guess so," Walt said slowly, flipping through the pages of his book once more. "Go home and get some sleep. I'll be talking to you later." He rose and prepared to leave, but he paused at the door. "Sorry about that knife wound, Brian."

"Thanks. It's nothing, though."

I waited a few minutes until I was sure he was gone. Then I left the room, emerging into the nurse's station. I saw Tom Ferris standing in the corridor; he came over to me quickly. I also saw Duval sitting inconspicuously on one of the chairs at the far end of the waiting room. I motioned to him that I would be with him in a moment.

Ferris looked at me intently, concern on his face. "How are you?"

"Fine."

"I wish the hell you had let me send one of my operatives with you. This wouldn't have happened."

"Maybe. I met some pretty professional customers. If your man had tagged along, there might be two corpses out on that street in Chevy Chase now."

The nurse was standing beside me, and she wanted me to fill out some forms or something. I asked Tom to give her the data. "I'll meet you outside. I've got to talk to somebody, and then we've got work to do."

I motioned to Duval, and he followed me out through the door of the emergency room. A police cruiser was just pulling in, and when it came to a halt, a police officer led a man with a bleeding head into the hospital. Nighttime in Washington.

Duval and I walked out toward the parking area, both of us remaining silent until we knew we were far enough from the building for anyone to overhear us. "You are all right, Brian?" he asked me.

I nodded yes. "I've got an important question to ask you. Think carefully now. Do you know anyone by the name of Therese Ballard?"

"Therese Ballard," he repeated slowly. "It is not an uncommon name, and perhaps I have met someone by that name. But I do not recall it. No, I do not know a Therese Ballard."

I looked at him carefully. He seemed to be telling the truth, but then evasion and discretion are the very special attributes of the diplomatic corps. He was a medium-built man in his late thirties, with rapidly thinning hair, and he spoke in a precise, clipped voice. I had worked with him on a number of deals, and we seemed to have gotten on together reasonably well. But, understandably, his basic loyalty was to the embassy, and not to me. There was no reason why he had to level with me if there were any embassy considerations to the contrary.

"And Therese Ballard is not employed by the embassy in any way?" I asked him.

"No, not at all. *Certainement.*"

It was, of course, the answer I expected. The answer I first realized on the sidewalk in Chevy Chase when I rolled over and saw Hervé's body.

"But who is Therese Ballard, and what does she have to do with this unfortunate incident?" Duval asked.

"I haven't got much time, but let me sketch it for you," I said, and briefly outlined the case—the Ballard woman's visit to my office, the assignment, the trip to Chevy Chase with Georges Hervé, the whole thing. "Now, that's all confidential," I told

Duval. "Only for you and the ambassador. I don't want this to get in the press."

"Oh, *mon Dieu,* no. We certainly do not want that in the press. But what does it all mean?"

I noticed that Tom Ferris had come out of the emergency-room door and was looking around for me. He finally saw me with Duval at the edge of the parking area, and I waved to him. "I don't know, but I'm sure as hell going to try and find out," I said to Duval. "But I've got one more question. Who is Georges Hervé? And please give it to me straight. I've been honest with you."

Duval rubbed his hand over his forehead. "Monsieur Hervé is a most respected financier and businessman. I did not know until this evening, until the ambassador telephoned me, that he was even in the United States."

"Do you know *why* he was in Washington?"

"No. I would suppose it has something to do with one of his innumerable financial … arrangements. He is engaged in many international cartels. But he is a man who flees publicity."

"That's the same story I heard," I observed dryly.

"It is a true story you heard, then."

"Okay. You tell the ambassador my story, and then see what you can dig up on Hervé's visit. I'll call you in the morning."

He hesitated. "Well, not at the embassy. Rather, allow me to call you. At your office."

I nodded agreement, and as I started to walk away from him, he said: "It is a most peculiar episode."

"Most peculiar," I answered.

Tom Ferris drove me downtown in his car, and on the way I recounted the entire story to him, beginning with the visit of the Ballard woman at my office. He listened intently, his lips pursed, a frown on his forehead. When I finished, we were driving along Rhode Island Avenue through moderately heavy traffic. He remained silent for a few moments, negotiating the car, thinking over what I had told him. Finally, he said: "And?"

"And—it means that I've been set up as a colossal pigeon."

"How do you figure that out?"

"Let's start at the beginning, or at least what I know of the beginning. This Hervé fellow is coming to Washington for some kind of deal. And let's work on the assumption for awhile that he is what he's supposed to be, a financier or businessman. Now, somebody—Therese Ballard, or more probably, whoever the hell she's working for—wants to get him. From what happened, we can see that maybe they wanted whatever he was carrying—the papers on him, the contents of his briefcase. And they probably wanted him killed, although that doesn't necessarily follow. So, their problem is to get a range finding on Hervé, intercept him at some propitious moment, and do their dirty work."

"And where do you come in?"

"I come in because there's a problem in locating this Hervé chap. Whoever he is, he certainly travels quietly and inconspicuously. The Ballard people weren't too sure where he was going while he was here. And they weren't even entirely certain he was going to stay at the Mayflower. And, remember, Duval just told me that he wasn't even aware of Herve's visit. Maybe the ambassador was. We don't know, but we'll find out. But, at any rate, the Ballard people certainly knew he was coming, and they wanted to get a bead on him. But keep in mind that this is an elusive fellow. So, they dream up a great solution, one involving the prize chump, Brian Petersen. On some pretext, they've got to find someone to follow Hervé around, keep him in view, and then when they want to strike, their pigeon will lead them directly to their mark."

"Brian Petersen and his chum, Tom Ferris," said Tom bitterly.

"To some extent, Tom. But I was the patsy. You were just following my directions. Somehow, they had heard of the little services I offered, and they probably checked me out and found that I was obtuse enough to be their pigeon. And it worked perfectly for them. Ballard comes to my office, representing herself as someone from the French Embassy. She's done her homework—she knows how I operate and what I can do. Some great undercover work there. She knew about my deals with Duval, and she knew how these assignments were usually conducted—by a lesser embassy figure, and with no direct contact with the embassy. Perfect. She saunters into my office, and I buy the whole package. And she even sweetens the whole deal with a great check—ten thousand, prepaid."

Tom whistled. "You didn't tell me that. Ten thousand."

"I told you I was getting well paid."

"Is the check good?"

"Sure. That was part of the act to make it look authentic. A cashier's check. That's why this deal was pretty important to somebody—they were willing to spend ten thou to have me act as their pigeon. Okay, so Ballard has me hired. I've bought the bit. Now she knows that Hervé will be trailed all the time he's in D.C. And remember that clever little routine of hers, the crap about not upsetting Hervé and not letting him know how we were shadowing him. I sure bought that like a dunce. Through me they can find out exactly where Hervé is at any time. And when he doesn't show up at the appointed arrival time, we even do the checking to find out when he's definitely arriving. No … wait a minute." I paused.

"What's the matter?"

"When she phoned me that day, she knew that his original flight plans had been cancelled. But I wonder if she knew that he was arriving the next day. I can't remember. Maybe I even fed that information to her. So, now they know that Hervé is in town and that he's staying at the Mayflower. All they have to do is arrange their hit. Their boy Brian Petersen will lead them right to him."

"Is that why they asked you to escort Hervé out to Chevy Chase?" Tom asked.

"Maybe, I don't know. There's a more plausible explanation for that. But let me get to that in a minute. Recall for a moment what had happened when Ballard phoned me this afternoon. I told her that Hervé was not leaving the hotel much, and maybe she already knew that. She probably did. They couldn't get a good shot at him. But I also gave her two beautiful pieces of information. One, that Hervé was going out to the suburbs, where it would be easier to get a shot at him. I think Miss Ballard, or whoever was doing the thinking for her, made a quick decision at that moment. She asked me to accompany him; in fact, she was pretty insistent about it. And again—damn it—I eagerly jumped at the bait. There are two reasons why she might have done that. And, for all I know, she may have done it for both of those reasons. Well, the first one, anyway. If I accompany Hervé, then he's somewhat easier to spot, because they've done their homework on me and presumably their thugs have pictures or descriptions of me. A big guy, identifiable, relatively easy to follow, as he accompanies their prey. Like a regular target finder. And, there's another part of that same first reason: They might have preferred to deal with me on that street in Chevy Chase, rather than with some private detectives who could presumably be working in a team and, therefore, put up a better defense."

Tom started to say something, but he quickly clamped his mouth shut.

"Don't say it, Tom. I know—you wanted your boys to tag along after me. And if they had, this wouldn't have happened. Maybe, maybe not."

"What's the other reason you think that the woman wanted you in Chevy Chase?"

"This," I said, and I picked up my torn and bloodied shirt, which I had brought with me and which was now on the seat of the car beside me. I unrolled it and held it out in front of me. "I don't know if you can see this while you're driving," I said, "but when you get a chance to look at it, you'll notice across the front a faint black smear. A lot of it is covered over by blood, but you can still see enough of it."

"What is it?" Tom asked.

"Grease paint, or burnt cork, or something like that. It's what those thugs had on their hands, and when I was tussling with one of them, some of it came off on my white shirt. Remember, the only part of their flesh that was exposed was their hands. They were wearing stocking masks down to their sweatshirts, and then those long sleeve jobs. They wanted to make it look like a regular mugging job by a gang of black men."

"Why?"

"To make it appear as un-newsworthy as possible."

"But, Brian, they must have considered that eventually you'd realize you'd been duped and that Therese Ballard was not part of the embassy. Why all the dramatics?"

"Not for me, Tom. Of course, they knew I'd realize that I'd been taken. They were counting on that. No, the grease paint was for the benefit of any bystanders who might happen to witness the—quote—mugging—unquote. But they were even lucky there. There were no witnesses to worry about. But, if there had been, then all they would have seen would have been four black men jumping two fairly prosperous-looking guys on the street. A robbery, and an unfortunate slaying in the process of defending ourselves. Another of those terrible stories you read in the newspapers. And they were counting on me to accept that version of it."

"Because they felt that was the easiest way out for you?"

"Exactly. I'm a two-bit lobby man who dabbles in this other stuff once in awhile. And, when I realized I'd been taken so gloriously, they were figuring that the last thing in the world I'd want would be any publicity about it. They were partly right about that, because I'm going to go through the motions of playing it their way. Even with the police. That's the story I had to tell Walt Comber. A regular mugging in the streets. And, I hope that if the papers pick it up, they'll treat it that way."

"But why would they care about covering your reputation?"

"They don't give a good goddam about me or my reputation, obviously. But they're working on the theory that *I* do. They're figuring that I'll just chalk this up to a bad scene, and try to forget about it as quickly as possible. And the easiest way to do that is to follow their script. That's to their advantage. Then the death of Georges Hervé can be attributed to an unfortunate but credible mugging on an American street, rather than a planned attack. The whole thing can be smoothed over much more easily that way. However, there's one little flaw in their plan...."

"Which is?"

"They didn't do a good-enough job of research on Brian Petersen. I'm not going to try and kick this under the rug."

"Maybe they know you better than you think they do."

"I doubt it. Take my knife wound, for instance. There was no necessity for knifing me, apart from some stupid revenge because I had gotten a slug into one of them. But I doubt that. These guys were too professional to waste time playing the revenge game. No, I think my stabbing was a calculated thing. On the one hand, it gave more credence to the mugging story. And, on the other, they just wanted to give me a prick with a knife, rather than let me have it like Hervé. Otherwise, there would have been another corpse out there, and much more publicity and many more questions asked. Besides, if I were left living, I could testify to the mugging scene. They were counting on that."

Ferris gestured with one hand toward my bandaged shoulder, now partly covered by my suit jacket. "I'd hardly call that a pin-prick."

"Sure it is," I said. "Beautifully planted, by a real pro, someone who's an expert with a knife. He stuck it right in the fleshy part of the shoulder, didn't cut any muscle, didn't touch any bones. It just bled a lot, which was the effect they wanted. My God, I was down on the ground when they stuck me, and if they wanted to do a good job they had a clean shot, not this little touch on the shoulder."

Tom maneuvered the car onto Connecticut Avenue, and in a few minutes he was pulling into the garage under my building. "Use my parking space," I told him. "I still have to retrieve my car from Chevy Chase. We'll get it later."

"What's the procedure?" Tom asked.

"I don't know. There's not much of a trail. But I'll start sniffing around and see what I can find."

As Ferris was turning off the ignition, he said: "Brian, I want to work with you on this."

"Sure, Tom. I'll need your help."

"No, I don't mean that way. You may think you've been taken for a patsy, but I feel the same way, too. They used me, maybe indirectly, but they nevertheless used me. And I don't like that, not at all. I want to work with you on a personal basis. No charge."

"I appreciate that, Tom, but no, I want to pay you something. We'll figure it out later. Don't forget, I still have that ten thou that Ballard gave me."

"That's blood money. I don't want any of that."

"No, that's my payoff money. To sweeten the deal. They figured I'd be happy to take the ten thou and run. Well, I'm going to take it, and I'm going to run—but not in the direction Therese Ballard wanted."

CHAPTER SIX

The lights were on in my office when we arrived, and Annie was there waiting for us. She put her hand over her mouth when she saw me, and cried: "Brian, what happened?"

I suppose I appeared fairly wretched—no shirt, the blood-splattered jacket, the torn trousers. And I recalled that, although I had been cuffed around a lot before, Annie had never seen the immediate aftermath. Her eyes were wide, and there was a terrified expression on her face.

"Just a little bump," I said, trying to calm her.

She noticed the bandage protruding from under my jacket. "Were you shot?" she asked.

"I got it in the more traditional way. A knife."

"But who——?"

"It's a long story, and I'll fill you in as we go along. But one of the main characters is our friend Therese Ballard."

"Therese Ballard?"

"Yes, our dear Joan of Arc—who is not a Joan of Arc. I doubt if she's even a Therese Ballard. But, at any rate, she *wasn't* from the French Embassy."

Annie's terrified expression gave way to one of puzzlement, then one resembling cold fury. "That woman!" she said.

"I need your help in identifying her, Annie. That's why I asked you to come down. I want to see if you and I can put together a description of her. Sorry to drag you out after supper."

"That's no problem. I'll enjoy doing this."

"Let's start on this Ballard woman," I said. "Did she seem like the real article to you, Annie?"

"She was the real article, all right. Very Frenchy."

"And you think she was authentically French?"

"She seemed so to me. Those were Parisian clothes she was wearing. She was very demanding, and she treated me with a superior, patronizing attitude. I didn't really care for her."

"I can't say that I'm wild about her, either," I said. "Okay, we've got an artist coming." I glanced at Tom.

"He should be here any minute," he said.

"We'll see if he can do a likeness from our descriptions, Annie. One more thing, though. Do you happen to have a note on that phone number Therese Ballard left for me this afternoon?"

"I can find it," Annie said, sliding behind her desk and pulling open one of the drawers.

"Good girl. Give it to Tom. And, in the meantime, I'm going to change out of these clothes."

I went into my office and opened a closet where I kept a few changes of clothes. I selected a clean shirt, a sports jacket, and a pair of slacks. I was washing up in the basin when Tom came in, a slip of paper in his hand. He read the number Therese Ballard had left for me this afternoon, and then said: "It's a Northwest number, probably residential."

"Get on it and find the address, will you?"

"I don't know if I can contact anybody this hour of night. The phone company doesn't give out that kind of information, you know. I'll have to pull some wires behind the scenes."

"Pull them, then," I said, drying myself off with a towel and reaching for the pair of slacks. "It will undoubtedly be a dead end. But we've got to try it. It's the only lead we have on Ballard at the moment."

There was another voice in the outer office, and a moment later Annie came in and told me that the artist was there. Tom went into the outer office to start working on the phone number, while Annie and I sat down with the artist. He was a lean, middle-aged man, and he seemed briskly proficient in his work. He pulled one of those face books out of his briefcase and began thumbing through it, as Annie and I gave verbal descriptions of Therese Ballard. The artist's book was divided into five flip-over sections—foreheads, eyes, noses, mouths, and chins. He started with the forehead and asked Annie and myself to select a forehead that most closely resembled that of the Ballard woman. Annie was much better at it than I, and after flipping around for a few moments among the foreheads, we finally found one that we both thought was right. Then the same procedure with the eyes. After about twenty minutes we had assembled a face that bore a fair resemblance to that of Therese Ballard.

"I'm not satisfied yet," Annie said, a frown on her forehead. "The eyes and the chin don't fit together somehow."

"Maybe I can capture it in a sketch," the artist said, pulling a large drawing pad out of his brief case. He laid the pad on my desk, and immediately next to it the facial identity book, which was now arranged to the composite of the various facial parts we had suggested to him. With amazing dexterity, he lightly traced a pencil drawing of the composite, bringing it into more proportion and symmetry. Annie still wasn't satisfied, and she suggested more changes to him. He rubbed out a line here and there, drew in other ones, accentuated a few of the characteristics, and astonishingly a reasonably good likeness of Therese Ballard began to emerge. Finally, he asked me if I agreed with the drawing.

"The eyes," I said, "they look too bland. They were sharper, more intense. Perhaps if they were a little more narrow."

The artist worked around the eyes with his pencil until I felt he had more faithfully captured the intensity of the Ballard woman. "Now," he said, "let me try a final sketch and see what that does for you." On a fresh piece of paper, he began to draw a new picture from the model of his first one. This one was drawn more carefully, but still with that same speed. When he was finished I felt we had a working likeness of the Frenchwoman who had visited my office a few days ago.

I held the picture up and examined it carefully. "Yeah, that's the bitch," I said. "Now, all we have to do is find her."

I thanked the artist for his time and cooperation, and Annie took the sketch out to the duplicating machine to make extra copies. By that time, Tom was back in the office with the address of the number from which Ballard had phoned me.

"I had to go all the way to a vice-president of the phone company," he complained, "a fellow I had worked with in the old days at the bureau in connection with some wiretapping stuff."

"But he gave it to you."

"Reluctantly. I owe him a favor now. The phone is listed at an address in Foggy Bottom. A private residence. There are two phones listed there," Tom said, consulting a note he had written. "One for a Mrs. Loretta Stone. That one was installed fourteen years ago. And a second one for a Miss Therese Ballard, and that one was installed ten days ago."

"Sounds like a woman who takes in boarders, doesn't it? Well, let's go over there and see what we can find."

"You don't expect to find that dame sitting there waiting for you, do you?" Tom said disdainfully.

"No, she's probably far gone by now. But maybe we can find something to pick up the trail."

Annie returned to the office with about a dozen duplicated copies of the artist's rendition of Therese Ballard. I folded two of them, inserted them in my pocket, and handed a number of them to Tom. "If my guess is right," I told him, "that gal is making tracks to get out of town. Can you get some of your men to work the airports, using those pictures?"

"All three airports?"

"Dulles and Friendship, especially. Have them take a close look at the international flights since, say, eight thirty this evening. I have a hunch that Ballard and company are winging back to Europe. But you might as well check out National Airport, too."

Tom used the phone on my desk, and in a few minutes he was able to tell me that he could arrange it. "I can now make use of the man over at the Mayflower," Tom said dryly.

"I'd forgotten about him," I said.

"He checked in with the office a few minutes ago. Says the police are in Hervé's room, going through it, and he wants to know what the hell's going on."

"I hope he can get out of there without being spotted by the police."

"I think he can," Tom said. "But I'll have to get these pictures of Ballard over to my office right away."

Annie, who had been standing in the doorway listening to us, said: "I'll take them over for you."

"Fine," I said. "That'll save us time. We can get moving right away to Foggy Bottom."

"For God's sake, be careful, will you?" Annie said apprehensively.

"Don't worry, sweets," I said, smiling. "The Ballard gang has gotten their shot at me. Next time it's my turn."

With Tom driving, we easily located the address in Foggy Bottom. It was one of a row of white-stoned Federal-styled buildings, two stories high. The time was ten o'clock, and the houses were all lighted, including the one we were looking for, number 206. We stood outside for a moment, and Tom said: "How do you want to handle this?"

"Let me do the talking," I said. "Follow my lead."

There was no doorbell, only a bronze knocker on the door, and I lifted it and rapped twice. I could hear a television playing from inside. After a few moments the door opened on a crack, and from behind a chain lock a middle-aged woman peered out at me.

I was still undecided as to how I was going to handle this, but the woman's puzzled and somewhat frightened expression gave me my lead. I decided to play it according to my assumptions of what Therese Ballard had done after the mugging earlier this evening. "Excuse us for bothering you at this late hour," I said. "We're acquaintances of Therese Ballard."

"Yes?" the woman asked uncertainly from behind the chain, shifting her gaze from myself to Tom. Ferris was standing slightly to my right, his hands hanging loosely at his side. His jacket was unbuttoned, and I knew that he was wearing a shoulder holster. He appeared casual and relaxed, but, of course, he was carefully poised to go for that pistol with lightning speed, if necessary.

"She's been rooming here, I understand, and now that she's departed, her room is vacant," I said.

The woman seemed to relax somewhat, but didn't unfasten the chain. "Yes, that was sudden," the woman said. "Left this afternoon. Said she was unexpectedly being transferred to Los Angeles."

"That's what she told us. It came up rather quickly. Have you rented her room yet?"

"Why, no. I was going to place an ad in the paper tomorrow. It all happened so suddenly."

"That's why we're here. We'd like to talk to you about the possibility of renting it."

"Well, I'm sorry," she answered. "I'd only rent it to a woman. I'm a widow, and I live alone. I've been renting that room to girls for a number of years. Usually working girls."

"Oh, it's not for me. It's for my younger sister. A girl just out of high school. Coming to work for the government." I was doing this badly, and I now regretted I had followed this tack. But I was into it now.

"Have her come around and see me tomorrow, then," the woman answered. She emphasized the "tomorrow."

"She's not arriving in town until the day after tomorrow. But I fairly well know what she's looking for, and I thought if we could take a look at the room right now we could almost make a decision. We'd pay you a small retainer, contingent upon your interview with her. And that way you could save yourself the bother and expense of inserting the ad in the paper." It didn't sound very convincing, and I could sense that Tom was becoming uneasy beside me.

I was considering the possibility of changing my tactic and telling this woman some small part of the actual story about Therese Ballard, enough to allow us to obtain a look at her room, when she suddenly said: "Do you have any identification?"

Good. She was, surprisingly, taking the bait. I produced a business card from the old billfold I had picked up at my office, a billfold into which I had stuffed some more cash and some new business cards. The woman accepted it across the chain, looked at it carefully for a few moments, and then slipped open the chain and pulled back the door. A small dog, a black terrier, crouched behind her and growled menacingly, and she whispered at it: "Quiet, Dodger!"

The woman began to chat volubly at us as she led us upstairs to the second floor. The usual sales pitch. The room was good; the rent was relatively inexpensive; the location was convenient. I pretended to listen attentively. At the rear of the upstairs hall, the woman opened a door and gestured into it. I entered, and Tom followed me immediately. A simple room, with a single bed against the far wall, and one easy chair, and a desk and chair. Tom moved casually around the room, as if he were trying to decide if it would be suitable for my sister. But I knew he was carefully examining it with his professional eye. He walked over to the window, touched the curtains lightly, then went over to the desk, laying his hand casually on it. He caught my eye. "Very clean," he said, meaningfully. He was telling me, of course, that there was no hope of raising any latent fingerprints from that surface.

"That Miss Ballard was a very neat person," the woman said brightly. "My, she even cleaned this room thoroughly before she left this afternoon. Not many of them do that."

"I guess not," Tom said dryly. He took a long, sweeping look around the room, and then shook his head. He placed a hand over his mouth, feigning a yawn. "Think I'll wait for you down in the car, Brian, I can let myself out."

He thumped down the stairs, and in a few seconds we heard the front door slam behind him. I knew that he was checking something else outside, and he wanted me to detain the woman. I asked her some questions about the utilities, and she told me that the telephone was not included. Miss Ballard had installed that at her own expense, and it had been disconnected this afternoon. But the instrument was still there, and it could be easily connected again. I asked her if she allowed her boarders to entertain in the house. Not ordinarily. Oh, once in a great while, if there were out-of-town visitors, or something like that. Miss Ballard didn't have any visitors, then? Oh, no, she lived very quietly. Went out in the evenings, but she was usually home by ten or ten thirty.

I continued to push the Ballard subject, but the only other thing I was able to learn was that Ballard told the woman she was working for some French importing firm. Beyond that, the landlady seemed to know as little about her as I did. Finally, after ten minutes, when I thought Ferris had enough time, I reached into my pocket and withdrew one of the artist's pictures of Therese Ballard. I wanted a positive identification.

"Is this the woman we're talking about?" I asked. "Your recent boarder, Therese Ballard?"

The woman's eyes narrowed suspiciously, and she turned her gaze from me to the picture. She nodded her head wordlessly in affirmation. "You're policemen, aren't you?" she said apprehensively.

"Not policemen, private detectives."

"And you're looking for Therese Ballard. What's she done?"

"Nothing," I said soothingly. "We only want to ask her some questions. Get some references from her about business people. Something to do with a business merger."

The woman appeared unconvinced. "I don't want any trouble. I've never had any trouble with the police."

"You won't have any trouble with the police. They won't bother you. This is strictly a private business arrangement."

She started to move toward the door, plainly wanting to get rid of me now. I thanked her for her time, and handed her a twenty-dollar bill. "For your inconvenience," I told her. She shook her head, refusing it. But I laid it down on the desk as I left the room.

Tom was waiting for me in the car when I emerged from the house. The engine was running, and he had the air-conditioner working full force. As I opened the car door, he offered me a cigarette, and after I had lighted it we sat there discussing our inspection of Therese Ballard's recent apartment.

"Clean as a whistle," Tom said. "She went over that whole place with a cloth of some kind. Rubbed out every possible kind of fingerprint. I think you're dealing with a real pro, Brian."

"That I'm aware of."

"There's only one little thing I picked up, and that's not much," he said, reaching into his pocket and withdrawing a matchbook cover. "I went down into that alley behind the houses, and rummaged through the trash barrel in back of number 206. Sometimes you pick up a lot of interesting things there. It seems that the resident of 206 is pretty fond of TV dinners. A lot of old tin-foil serving plates in the barrel. And this one matchbook cover."

He handed it to me, and I saw that it was from a small French restaurant on 12th Street at which I had eaten a number of times. "It's probably hers," I said.

"I'd imagine so. I don't think the TV dinners and the French restaurant go together."

"Okay," I said, putting the matchbook cover into my pocket. "It's not much help, but it's all we have so far." I leaned back and rested my head on the seat with my eyes closed. "So what have we learned?" I said. "Therese Ballard rented this apartment two weeks ago. Told the landlady that she was working for some type of French firm. Had a phone installed. Then today, she suddenly tells her she is being transferred to Los Angeles. I don't believe that Los Angeles bit. She was probably going in exactly the opposite direction. But she's gone—cleanly."

"I can check that phone tomorrow and see if she made any long-distance calls on it. But I doubt it. She seems too smart for that."

"Yeah," I said moodily.

"Want to call it a night?" Tom asked, shifting the automatic transmission into the drive position.

"We're just beginning. Let's drive out to Chevy Chase. I'll show you where I got zapped."

CHAPTER SEVEN

We drove out to Chevy Chase, the second time I had been there that evening.

The main difference, however, was that during this trip I was considerably more alert and attentive.

The street on which the attack had taken place was now deserted. The police were gone, the crowds dispersed, and, of course, Hervé's body had been removed. The only car parked on the side of the street where I had been stabbed was my own black Oldsmobile. I noted that the lights were still burning in the house where Hervé had intended to visit earlier this evening.

Ferris took a flashlight from his glove compartment, and I pointed out the exact spot on the sidewalk. He probed it with his flashlight, illuminating the area. Someone had evidently hosed down the sidewalk, but you could still see the faint outline of the chalk mark that had been drawn around Hervé's body, and also a number of brownish stains that the spraying water had not completely eradicated.

I tapped one of the stains with my foot. "That's some of the precious Petersen blood," I said to Tom.

Tom held his flashlight beam on it for a moment, and then ran it over to the chalk marks. "Your friend Hervé lost a hell of a lot more than you did. Do you think they killed him instantaneously?"

I studied the location for a minute. "No, of course not," I said. "I gave him a shove toward that grassy area there, and that's where the first guy hit him. Then … I kicked him off Hervé, and Hervé must have started to get up, because he ended up over here a few feet on the paved area. I didn't see that."

"Where was the position of the man you shot?"

"Over there someplace." Tom flashed his beam in the direction I was pointing, and about a dozen feet away we could see another brownish stain.

"That's also a pretty good one. I'd say a distance of ten to fourteen feet. Fairly good range for that little .32. I'll bet the fellow you shot isn't feeling too good right now."

"I hope not."

Tom continued to study the area, walking back and forth across it, stooping over to examine something more closely. But he was unable to find anything new that could be of any help to us. "I'd say that was a beautifully executed hit," Tom said. "How long do you think your assailants were following you?"

"They probably picked me up as I left my own office, and then followed me down to the Mayflower. And, when I came out with Hervé, they tagged right along and waited for a suitable place."

"And you didn't catch the tail."

"Missed it completely. The first thing I noticed was the car pulling up behind me as we were parking. And at that, I only saw the one man sitting in the car."

"You're slipping, Brian." He cast the beam of his flashlight around for one final look. "Nothing more here. Another dead end."

"Let's keep plugging, Tom. We'll find something." I gazed up at the house where Hervé was to have visited. "Since we're not picking up anything at the one end, maybe we should try the other end. I'd like to have a talk with a man named Metivier."

"Metivier?" Ferris asked, pulling out his notebook.

"Alphonse Metivier, if I remember correctly. That's the man Walt Comber told me Hervé was on his way to see," I said, pointing to the house on the top of the rising lawn.

When I rang the bell, there was no answer, despite all the lights, and so I pressed it firmly, holding it for the best part of a minute. Finally, the door opened on a crack, and I was peering again at another middle-aged woman over a chain. It was becoming the night of chains. I told her I wanted to see Monsieur Metivier, and she firmly informed me that (a) Monsieur Metivier never sees anyone without an appointment, and (b) that Monsieur Metivier furthermore never, never receives anyone at this hour of the night. I started to speak in my pigeon French and inserted my card through the chain, telling her that I was the man who was injured on the street a few hours ago when Monsieur Hervé was killed, and would she please tell Monsieur Metivier that I only wanted a few minutes of his time to discuss this awful tragedy. That got to her, and she said she would take my message to Monsieur Metivier. However, she firmly closed the door when she left. A minute later the chain from inside was loosened, and the door was opened by a tall, erect man in his late fifties. He was wearing a smoking jacket and had a compelling air of distinction about him, but nevertheless there was an unmistakable look of fright and confusion in his eyes. I thought I recognized him as one of the people who had been standing near Hervé's corpse on the street a few hours ago.

"I am Alphonse Metivier," he said, opening the door. He was holding my business card in his hand, and he glanced at it. "And you are Mr. Petersen?"

I said that I was, and I introduced Tom as a business associate of mine. He invited us into his study, a book-lined room with heavy walnut furniture. He asked us if we would like some cognac, and when we agreed, he poured us two small glasses from a decanter that was sitting on a sideboard. He also poured one for himself, then settled into one of the chairs and shook his head. "I do not know what to say. It is terrible, terrible. Monsieur Hervé murdered on my very doorstep." He took a deep swallow of his cognac, as if he were trying to eradicate the scene from his mind. He placed his glass on a small table beside the large wing chair in which he was sitting, and looked intently at me. "Ah, Mr. Petersen, you must excuse my manners. I am so upset. I did not inquire about your injury."

"A minor one," I said.

"I saw you during that dreadful scene on the sidewalk, but you were being attended to and I felt I should stay with the body of poor Hervé. There was so much bewilderment. I was sitting here in my study, waiting for Hervé to arrive, and then I heard all that shouting on the street. When I went outside I saw that horrible tableau. Monsieur Hervé lying there in that pool of blood, and yourself bleeding, too. There was so much bewilderment, I did not know what to do. They took you away in the ambulance, and I waited until the police officers had removed Monsieur Hervé's body. Then I phoned the embassy. They said they would talk on the wireless to France and inform Monsieur Hervé's family and firm of this unbelievable tragedy. Right in front of my home." He took another sip of cognac. "I was not aware that you were to accompany him this evening, Mr. Petersen. You are a business associate of his?"

"A very casual acquaintance," I said carefully. "I was accompanying Monsieur Hervé tonight because he was unfamiliar with the city."

"Ah, yes," Metivier said. "The city. There is so much violence and theft downtown, and now it is even spreading out here. And it had to happen tonight. Of all nights. When the distinguished Monsieur Hervé is coming to visit *my* home."

"You knew Hervé well?" I asked, leading him cautiously.

"I have never met him before. We have corresponded, and I have done a number of services for him during the past two years. I am an attorney, in the field of international law. Most of my services for his firm have been done with ... with underlings or with his attorneys in Paris. Monsieur Hervé is a man who very much remains in the background."

"And yet he came to America on this negotiation?" I felt that Metivier's anguish was genuine, and, therefore, that I'd be able to draw some information out of him if I could gently give him a release and let him talk as a sort of verbal catharsis.

"Tonight he was coming to the house of Alphonse Metivier," he said, somewhat proudly. "This was to be one of his major transactions, and he wanted to do it personally."

"It was strange he changed his travel plans at the last moment, wasn't it?" I said guilefully.

"It was, was it not?" Metivier answered in his French accent. "We had been corresponding all spring about his visit, which was originally scheduled for last evening. I was to have arranged a meeting here at my house between himself and an American attorney. And then, yesterday I received a cablegram informing me that he would not be here until tonight, and that I should inform the American attorney not to attend. We had other details to iron out first."

"Yes, strange, isn't it?" I mused for the benefit of Metivier. "Do you happen to still have that cablegram?" I asked.

"I do. It was sent here to my home." Metivier rose and went over to his desk, and returned handing me a cablegram. It said substantially what Metivier had said. Part of the cablegram read: *Cancel meeting with Standish. Will contact him after arrival.*

I handed the cablegram back to him. "Monsieur Metivier," I said deliberately, "what was the nature of Hervé's business in this country?"

A wary look came into his eye. "Oh, Mr. Petersen, I would not be at liberty to tell you that. It would be a violation of my professional ethics. The confidence of a client."

"But it was a business transaction of some sort?"

Metivier was on his guard now, and I knew I was not going to obtain any more easy information from him. "I think that would be obvious," he said guardedly. "I was retained to be his legal adviser in the United States. To advise him in the legal aspects of his negotiations with the principals in this transaction. Actually, I know very few details of the transaction myself. Monsieur Hervé was being most secretive about this matter, particularly in our correspondence of the past month."

"And Mr. Standish is the American attorney?"

Metivier suddenly realized that he had supplied too much information. He took a hurried gulp of his cognac and said, "Yes," almost inaudibly.

I took the picture of Therese Ballard from my pocket and showed it to him. "Do you know this woman?" I asked.

He studied it carefully for a few moments, and then shook his head slowly. "No, I am afraid I do not. Does she have some connection with Monsieur Hervé's business?"

"I'm not quite sure."

We talked for a few more minutes, but I felt there was nothing further to be learned here and so we excused ourselves. Metivier himself accompanied us to the door, and as we were about to leave, he shook his head sadly. "I am afraid I shall not sleep well tonight."

"Drink some more cognac," I said kindly.

"I am sure I will drink much cognac. It is a tragedy for everybody. For Monsieur Hervé, of course. And for me, too. Monsieur Hervé was the most important client I ever had, and tonight might have been the beginning of something…." His voice trailed off, and he waved his hand aimlessly in the air.

Tom and I walked down to my parked Olds and I asked him: "What do you think?"

"It sounds straight," Tom said. Tom had not participated in my interview with Metivier, but I was glad to have him there. He is extremely good at the discernment of people, and he could sit back and study the Frenchman while I did the talking.

"You believe his story?" I asked.

"I'm inclined to. He seemed to be telling it straight, with all the proper emotion. If he wasn't straight, he should be back in France making films for the Cannes Festival."

I exhaled a deep breath. "I tend to agree with you. Although it doesn't help us much. However, we did get a few little pieces of information."

"Nothing that's going to lead us to your friend, Therese Ballard, though."

"You never can tell. Does the name Standish mean anything to you?"

"It sounds like Roger Standish. He's an international lawyer. Strictly top drawer. Has a big office on Pennsylvania Avenue."

"I think I'll pay a little visit to Mr. Standish tomorrow. But let's make one more stop tonight. Henri's restaurant on 12th Street. Let's see if your matchbook cover can give us a lead."

I had my hand on the door of my car and was about to open it when Tom stopped me. "Let me take a look at your car first." He slid behind the seat and, reaching over very carefully, ran his hand along the underside of the dashboard. Then he reached under the accelerator, pulling it up gently. He got out of the car and opened up the hood and began to peer inside, touching his hand to various parts of the motor.

"Looking for a bomb?" I said, amusement in my voice.

Tom, his face intent, continued his examination. "Perhaps. I think it's time you'd better start taking the obvious precautions and look over your shoulder regularly." He apparently didn't find what he was looking for, and so he closed the hood, an expression of concentration on his face.

"Satisfied?" I asked.

"Not yet." He walked around the car to the rear bumper and studied it for a moment. Then, kneeling down on one knee, he placed his hand under the chassis. A moment later he tugged at something and stood up, a small triumph on his face. He was holding a small metal box in his hand, the size of a package of cigarettes. It had been taped under the chassis of my car.

"Electronic device?" I asked.

Tom nodded his head. "Your assailants didn't have to trail you too closely. Sometime today probably, one of them fastened this under your car, and they had an electronic beam on you."

"But they'd need two cars to do that, wouldn't they?"

"For the best result. Oh, you can do a lot with one car. They pick up the beam from this little bug on the machine in their car and they can get a fairly good idea of your general direction and location. Of course, if you have two cars spread out, it's perfect. They both pick up your beam, and at the vector point where the beams cross, there you are exactly. I'd suppose these pros used two cars, with dual machines, radio intercom, the works."

"Son of a bitch," I said.

I drove my own car downtown, while Tom followed me in his. It was close to midnight now, and the traffic was extremely light. On 12th Street there was practically no traffic at all, a usual phenomenon here in the city now. With the threat of violence on the streets, the remembrance of past urban riots, and the rising crime rate, people were becoming increasingly disenchanted with the downtown area after dark. What they formerly could do down here in the evenings, they now have learned to do in their suburban areas. Theaters, restaurants, stores—all of these are now available in suburbia. And thus, when the male wage earner returns to his suburban environment at five o'clock in the afternoon, not to re-enter these urban areas until the next morning, the city then takes on an eerie and desolated character. Particularly affected by this social shift are the downtown restaurants.

The restaurant toward which we were driving was one I have patronized frequently. It was small, not particularly well-known, but it was authentically French. Not like those tourist traps with French names and menus and Greek waiters who pretend they are from Paris. The proprietor, Henri, was a busy little man with a gleaming bald head, and he greeted me warmly when we entered.

"Monsieur Petersen," he said. "Ah, the kitchen is closed, but we can do a little something for you."

It was almost midnight, and I remembered that I had not eaten dinner, but nevertheless I was not hungry. The attack, the excitement, the beginning of the chase, had, I suppose, masked my appetite. "I'm not hungry," I told Henri. "Your bar is still open, isn't it?"

"*Mais oui.* The usual for you? The Scotch with the piece of lime."

I nodded, and Henri asked Tom what he wanted. "Oh, I guess the same for me, but don't put the damn piece of lime in mine."

Henri himself brought the drinks to our table, and I asked him how his trade had been that evening. There were only a few tables occupied, but these were the last of the late-evening diners, leisurely finishing their meals. Henri spread his hands in a gesture of frustration. "It is adequate, but it is not really good," he said. "People are afraid of the city."

We talked for a few minutes about Henri's problems, and then I asked him if he could sit down for a moment because I needed his help with something. He glanced around the room, satisfying himself that the last of his customers were taken care of, and then drew a chair over to our table. I spread the picture of Therese Ballard on the tablecloth and asked him if he could identify the woman.

Henri laid his hand on the edge of the picture, studying it for a moment, and finally said: "*Coq au vin.* The lady who always orders the *coq au vin.*"

I looked at Tom. There was the beginning of a slight smile at the corner of his mouth. His matchbook cover had finally given us some kind of a lead.

"Who is she?" I asked Henri.

"I do not know. She has only been coming here for a few weeks, but she has been in here four or five times. And always the *coq au vin.* Uneducated palate."

"When was the last time she was here?"

Henri thought for a moment. "Yesterday, the day before yesterday, I am not sure."

"Was she alone?"

"A few times, but most often she was accompanied by a heavy-set man. Ah, he knew how to order from the menu."

"Was he French?"

"No. They both spoke to the waiters in French. She is French, and he speaks excellent French but with a slight accent. I would say middle European of some sort."

"You have any idea who he was?"

Henri shook his head. "The only time he has been in here is with the woman," he said, pointing to the picture.

"Embassy type, do you think?"

"Perhaps, but I do not think so. One evening it was raining and when the man brought his car around to the front, I accompanied the woman to the car with an umbrella. D.C. license plates, but a rented car. Henri notices these little details."

I continued to ask Henri questions, attempting to discover any more details he may have noticed, but that appeared to be the sum of the information he was able to offer us. We had another drink, and I asked Henri if he would supply his description of Ballard's companion to an artist, as Annie and I had done earlier this evening. Henri agreed, and Tom said he would bring the same artist to the restaurant tomorrow before it opened.

As we were leaving, I told Henri how sorry I was that his restaurant was not prospering as well as it should.

He smiled sadly. "The danger on the streets. *Oui, je suppose.* But for the true French cuisine, one should be willing to expose himself to a little danger."

Outside, Tom and I discussed the new information we had gleaned from Henri, but Tom was skeptical about the value of it. "I'll take the two artist's reconstructions—the one of Ballard, and the one of the man I get from Henri tomorrow—and spread them among some people around town who should know something," he said, "but I don't think anybody's going to be able to identify them. This has all the earmarks of out-of-towners coming in for a quick job, and then fleeing."

"Maybe. But we still have to touch all the bases."

Tom yawned, placing his hand over his mouth, and I told him to go home and get some sleep.

"Yeah," he said willingly. "One last thing, though. Let me check back at the office and see if we made any identifications at the airports."

There was a lighted phone booth at the corner, and Tom made his call there, while I stood beside my car and smoked a cigarette. When Tom returned, he told me that his operatives had been checking with airline agents at the three airports, but nobody had identified Therese Ballard as having boarded a flight today.

"I'm going to have somebody fly copies of the picture up to New York," he said, "and I'll have an agency up there do the New York airports for us"

"Good, Tom. Pass the word around. I'm looking for little Miss *Coq au Vin* and her friends."

It was after one o'clock when I arrived home, and I went downstairs to pour myself one more Scotch. I was tired and my knife wound was throbbing, and I was having difficulty trying to sort it all out in my mind. There were so many unanswered questions. Who in God's name were these people who wanted to kill Georges Hervé? And why? Furthermore, why didn't they try to kill him in Paris, where presumably they would have an easier shot at him?

And I thought again of that briefcase he had been carrying. That had to be it. They not only wanted Hervé himself but they also wanted those papers he had been carrying. That's why they didn't just hit him at the airport or on a busy street. They wanted to isolate him in some quiet spot where they would be sure of snatching the briefcase without fear of being apprehended. And that's why they hired Brian Petersen to be their little homing pigeon to lead them right to Hervé for a perfect hit and heist.

Dammit, I thought with mounting anger, I was going to hunt down those bastards no matter where the trail led.

I suddenly remembered that the police still had my pistol, but I had another .32 here in the house. I went and got it, and laid it on the bar, a box of cartridges next to it. Then, carefully and methodically, I field-stripped it, examining each part and laying it on the bar. Next, I reassembled it, and pulled the trigger of the unloaded pistol a few times. It seemed to be working perfectly. Finally, I slowly loaded it with new shells.

CHAPTER EIGHT

Annie was sitting behind her desk when I arrived at the office the following morning, reading the *Washington Post* and the brief account of Georges Hervé's killing.

"Not much of a story," she said.

"That's fine with me," I said. Yesterday had been a heavy news day, with a major airline crash in Mexico, and the outbreak of some small fighting in the Middle East, and the Hervé story was buried back on page four. The head stated simply: MAN KILLED ON CHEVY CHASE STREET. The two-paragraph story followed the account I had given the police. Hervé was identified as a French tourist, and I as a local lobbyist.

"Annie, there's an attorney, Roger Standish, on Pennsylvania Avenue. See if you can get an appointment for me this morning. Tell him it's urgent and has to do with Georges Hervé. You can even tell him I was with him last night when he was killed, if you have to."

I went into my office, and a few seconds later Annie buzzed me on the intercom to tell me that Duval from the French Embassy was on the line.

"Good morning, Brian, are you all right today?" he said. I could hear the sounds of traffic in the background, and I knew he was calling from a public booth someplace out on the street.

"I'm fine, Jacques."

"The ambassador wishes me to express his regrets for the injuries you suffered last night."

"Thanks." It was the old diplomatic protocol.

"Have you learned anything else about this unfortunate affair?" he asked.

"I think I have a drawing of this Therese Ballard. I'm going to send it over to you by special messenger." He hesitated a moment, and I added: "Don't worry, it will be in an unmarked envelope. Just a picture inside. I want you to see if you can identify that woman."

"*Bien.* The ambassador would also like to ask you a favor."

"All right, but first I want some information. Did the ambassador know that Hervé was coming to Washington?"

"The ambassador told me last night that he only had a general knowledge of Georges Hervé's visit, but no specifics. The first time he learned of his actual presence in the city was when that lawyer in Chevy Chase, Metivier, phoned that Hervé was lying dead on the street outside his house. And, then, *mon Dieu,* what a night! Since Monsieur Hervé was such an important man, the ambassador called the White House, and arrangements were made for an immediate autopsy so the body could be returned home right away. We had the autopsy about midnight, and then a funeral director took the body out to the airport. I accompanied it, and it was put on an early morning flight for Paris. I did not get much sleep last night."

"Does the ambassador know the purpose of Hervé's visit to America?"

"He did not discuss it with me, Brian."

"But do you think he knows?"

"I have no way of knowing that."

I had an extremely strong suspicion that they knew a hell of a lot more than they were willing to tell me. "Okay," I said. "What's the ambassador's favor?"

"He is extremely distressed that we were not able to return Monsieur Hervé's papers with him to Paris. If you could somehow locate that briefcase and return it to us, we would appreciate it. And we would express our gratitude—materially."

"Sure. If I find the Ballard woman, I might also find the briefcase. You can have the briefcase, and I'll take Ballard."

"*Merci bien.* I'll phone you back after we examine that picture."

A few minutes later, Annie buzzed me to say that she had arranged an appointment for me with Roger Standish at eleven o'clock. She also told me that there was a man on the phone who wanted to speak to me about the killing of Georges Hervé. He wouldn't give his name, and Annie thought he might be some crank who read the story in the morning paper. Nevertheless, I told Annie to put him on.

"Mr. Petersen," the voice said. "You are engaging in very dangerous activities. I urge you to stop immediately." The voice was heavily accented—European, perhaps Slavic.

"Who is this?"

"You were paid to perform a specific assignment. To escort Monsieur Hervé around town. That assignment is completed. Forget about Hervé now."

"Why should I?"

"Because you have been paid very well for your assignment. Furthermore, your life was spared last night in Chevy Chase. So, you have the money and your life. Go away, take a vacation, relax. But if you persist in this Hervé matter, you will be killed. Take my word for it."

"Go to hell. You can tell Therese Ballard and her friends——"

But the phone had clicked dead at the other end.

I leaned back in my chair and lighted a cigarette. So, they knew I was coming after them. They knew I was digging into this Hervé affair. But how? It was only a little over twelve hours after Hervé had been killed. Maybe they had Therese Ballard's apartment staked out and saw me snooping around there. Or, maybe they saw me return to Metivier's late last night, or stop at Henri's restaurant. Or, perhaps they had picked up the word that Tom Ferris was spreading around.

Perhaps even somebody like Jacques Duval might have tipped them off, playing both ends against the middle. Hell, from this point on I wasn't going to trust anybody completely.

Furthermore, I really didn't give a damn that they knew I was trying to track them down. It was apparently making them nervous, and I rather enjoyed that.

I walked out to Annie's office and asked her to send a copy of the Ballard drawing to Duval at the embassy. I told her I was going over to see Standish and would return later.

The elevator in my building goes right down to the garage level, and I was alone when I finally arrived there. There are some attendants up at the top of the ramp, up at the street level, and they will run down and get your car for you. But many of us in the building prefer to save time by parking and retrieving our own cars. My Olds was parked way down at the far end, and I walked through the now-deserted garage past the rows of parked automobiles.

I had just reached my car when I heard the step behind me. Instinctively, I whirled, my hand going for the .32 in the belt holster at my spine. But I was a second too late. As I came around, I was face-to-face with a man holding a .45 automatic on me.

"Hold it," he said, before I could get my pistol out.

And I knew what had happened—he had been crouched behind a parked car someplace, and when I walked by, he stepped out behind me, his pistol leveled right at my back.

"Hands on your head, Petersen," he said, and I complied.

He was a young man, perhaps someplace in his late twenties, wearing a blue-denim jacket. His face was thin, and pockmarked, and he had an unhealthy pallor about him. That pasty complexion was quite identifiable—the unmistakable mark of a person who had recently been in prison. But he had a good build, and I noticed those powerful-looking arms and those large hands.

And I immediately noticed something else, too—wrapped around the knuckles of his left hand was a savage-looking pair of brass knuckles, topped with tiny spikes along the upper ridge. Those knuckles could break a man's jaw in a dozen places, and tear his face to shreds.

"Turn around again," he told me, and as I turned my back to him he lifted the .32 from my holster, and threw it away. I could hear it clattering across the concrete surface someplace behind me.

"Now," he said, his voice rising in anticipation, "turn around toward me again, Petersen."

As I turned to face him, I wasn't too worried about that .45 for the moment. Had he wanted to use it, he could have shot me in the back. No, this was to be a beating with those knuckles. That realization gave me a slight advantage. At the instant I turned to face him he brought his left hand around in a wide arc, aiming dead for the center of my face. I managed to duck the blow slightly, but he still caught me a glancing blow high on the forehead.

I reeled backward under the impact of the blow, but he came right after me. However, he appeared to be somewhat disconcerted now. He apparently had planned to deck me with that first blow, and I think he had intended to shift the knuckles to his right hand, and then give me a thorough going-over. He seemed to be having trouble measuring me for a blow with his left hand now. He swung, and missed. I stepped in closer, but then he caught me with those knuckles right in the pit of the stomach. I grunted in pain, and fell back again.

And he came right after me again.

But this time as those knuckles flashed in the air, I grabbed his left wrist and jerked with all my might. He was too powerful to get up in the air over my shoulder, but I did manage to hold on and swing him around in a wide arc. And then I let go, slamming him up against a parked car. He hit with a loud crash, and the .45 went flying out of his hand, but he was back on his knees instantly, glaring at me, the knuckles still attached to his left hand.

He charged at me, measuring me with those knuckles, but then he did a smart thing—he pulled the punch, and struck me a vicious right across the bridge of my nose. Instantly, blood spurted out, and I tried to keep my vision clear. He tried to follow it up with a left, but I moved in close, grabbing him around the waist and holding on. We struggled for a few seconds, as he tried to get free and line me up for another punch.

I suddenly released him, and hit him with two fast blows to the face, a quick left and a powerful right. He grunted, but he didn't go down. Instead, he came at me again. He seemed to have forgotten about his left hand and the knuckles for the moment because he was swinging round-house rights. One caught me high on the cheekbone, and I almost went down. But I stayed in there, trading punches, and one got him right on the bridge of the nose and I could hear the cartilage crack as the punch landed.

He stepped back, and we circled for a moment, and now he seemed to be doing more thinking. He came at me, his left hand with the knuckles extended in front of him. I charged, flinging myself at him in a flying tackle, going in low under the left hand. I hit him slightly above the knees and held on as he toppled over. We rolled over, and he managed to bring his knee up, catching me in the stomach. I had to release him, and he scrambled to his feet. As I got up on one knee, he kicked me squarely in the chest. I went over on my back, but I purposefully kept rolling to get away from him.

I must have rolled over four or five times until I hit a wall, and then I started to get to my feet. But my attacker had not come immediately after me. He was standing some ten feet away, and now I could see that he had transferred the knuckles to his right hand. There was a slight smirk on his face as he started to move slowly toward me.

Then I saw it, lying on the ground, some four or five feet away—my .32 revolver.

I made a dive for it at the instant my attacker started his move toward me. He apparently saw the pistol, too, because he began to run at me. I managed to get the pistol in my hand, and still on the ground, I rolled over.

The attacker was about three or four feet away now, coming directly at me, those knuckles aimed directly for my face. I squeezed the trigger once. The trajectory path of the bullet was upward, and I think the shell entered directly under his chin and then coursed on up through his head someplace. He continued to run for another step or so, and then he crashed into the wall, banged backward and fell to the ground. He lay there, lifeless.

I rolled him over, and his eyes looked up at me in the dull stare of death.

For almost a minute I stood there, waiting to see if the shot would bring anybody running, but apparently, with all the traffic outside, the one shot went unnoticed. I was there alone in the garage with a corpse. And I had to make some quick decisions.

Obviously, this fellow had been hired by the Ballard people. He knew my name, and he had been staked out here near my car. There had been no attempt at robbery; rather, he was trying to give me a complete beating. It was to be another warning from the Ballard people to lay off the Hervé affair. More than that, it would put me out of action for quite awhile. That fellow with the knuckles could have broken my jaw in a number of places, and ripped my face to pieces, and he probably would have kicked my ribs to bits, too. I would have been in the hospital for months, maybe years, and that would have taken care of Brian Petersen. In some ways, that would have been more effective than killing me, because another murder might have raised a lot of questions in the authorities' minds. Furthermore, by the time I got out of the hospital, the Ballard people would be far gone and perhaps I might have lost any enthusiasm for the whole thing.

I went through the pockets of the corpse, hoping to find some identification, but I couldn't find much. No driver's license, no Social Security card. But, in his hip pocket, I did find a letter addressed to Fred Wilkes at a street number near Union Station. It sounded like a boarding house. The letter was from a girl in Philadelphia, and she wanted to know when Fred was coming to visit her again.

Never, baby, never, I thought.

I also found five new one-hundred-dollar bills in his pocket. And that confirmed what I thought was Fred Wilkes's role in this matter. He was a local thug, probably an ex-con, who had been hired by some of the Ballard people to give me a crippling beating. There was no use trying to follow up on Fred Wilkes, because he undoubtedly only had this single connection with the

Ballard people. For all I knew, the whole thing might have been arranged by telephone.

But I felt that I couldn't leave Fred Wilkes's corpse lying there in the garage under my building. When the body was finally discovered, some of those attendants upstairs might remember that I drove out of the garage shortly after Wilkes was killed. And that would bring Walt Comber on my trail again. I couldn't afford that. It would mean answering a lot of questions, and it would slow me down considerably. And I didn't want to waste time on the killing of a local thug—I wanted the boss of the operation.

I opened the trunk of my Olds and carefully lifted the corpse into it. There wasn't much blood on the ground, because Wilkes had died almost instantly, but what there was of it I wiped up with some rags. As I drove out of the garage, I looked at myself in the rear-view mirror. There were some small puncture wounds on my forehead where he had hit me that first glancing blow with the knuckles, and the blood from the nose punch had streamed down my face and all over my shirt. My suit was also ripped and torn in a number of places.

Driving at moderate speeds, I crossed the city, and then got out on Canal Road on the west side of Washington. When I found a fairly deserted stretch, I pulled over and waited until I was sure no cars were coming in either direction. Then I lifted the body out of the trunk, and threw it into a field by the road. I gunned the car, and pulled away quickly.

On the way back into town, I stopped at a garage and went into the bathroom. I washed up, stripped off my jacket and shirt, and put on a banlon shirt and golf jacket I had in the car. I had kept the letter from Fred Wilkes's body, and now I tore it in shreds and flushed it down the toilet. I had also kept the five hundred dollars, and I stuffed the money in my pants pocket.

That was the end of Fred Wilkes. Nice try, Ballard and Company.

I was late for my appointment with Roger Standish and I was hardly dressed properly for the office of a high-priced Washington attorney. But that really didn't make any difference, because Standish wasn't about to tell me what I wanted to know, anyway.

He was a large, heavy-set man in his late fifties, and he was cordial enough to me as he sat behind his massive mahogany desk in his office. He wanted to know about last evening, and I gave him the contrived newspaper story about a mugging on the street.

"And what was your relationship to Hervé?" he wanted to know.

"I was simply escorting him around town."

"I see," he said, his eyes narrowing, and I knew he didn't believe that.

"And what was *your* relationship to Hervé?" I asked.

"Purely professional. Hervé and I have been working together on a project for well over a year. We've met perhaps four or five times, and just last month I was in Paris to meet him."

"What was the project, Mr. Standish?"

"Oh, come, Mr. Petersen. You know I can't tell you that. I represent a number of American principals on a confidential business affair Hervé was negotiating. It would be highly unethical for me to reveal the nature of those negotiations to you."

"What's going to happen to those negotiations now?"

"God only knows. I've been on the phone to Paris this morning to Hervé's firm, but they're as confused as anybody else at the moment." He paused, eyeing me appraisingly. "One reason I was willing to see you on such short notice this morning, Mr. Petersen——"

"Yes?" I said. I knew what he was going to ask.

"Hervé was carrying some critically important business papers with him, and I understand his briefcase was taken during the killing last night. If you should recover that around town, I'd be happy to pay you a very handsome finder's fee for it."

"Sure," I said. There it was—that briefcase again. It was becoming the key issue in this strange affair. However, I doubted if it could be found anyplace around town by this time. I was sure that Ballard and her friends had spirited it far away during the past day.

I was feeling particularly frustrated when I left Standish's office. The lawyer wouldn't tell me the nature of Hervé's important business in the States, and the French Embassy, which apparently knew a lot about it, wasn't about to tell me, either. It was that damn international community in Washington composed of diplomats and embassy staffs and international businessmen. And it was a hell of a job to crack that impenetrable wall. The only crevice I knew was Stefan Meyner at the Swiss Embassy, an old friend of mine. Stefan was the only one in that whole international crowd whom I really trusted implicitly, and I knew he wouldn't mind receiving a call directly from me.

I called the Swiss Embassy from a pay phone booth, and when I told Stefan I had to see him right away, he agreed to meet me in a bar on M Street in Georgetown in a half-hour.

When Stefan entered the bar, I was sitting alone at a table in the rear, sipping a Scotch and lime. "Brian, are you all right? I read in the newspaper...."

"I'm fine, Stefan. Thanks for coming."

He was a spare man in his early forties, a career diplomat, with pale features, and a pleasant relaxed expression. Stefan had those polished, impeccable manners of people in the diplomatic corps, but beneath that necessary façade was a genuine person whom I had come to know and like over the years. As a matter of fact, he had been present at that party when I first met Marge years ago. He now ordered a Dubonnet while I proceeded to tell him the full and honest story of what had happened to me in the Hervé affair, omitting only my clash with the assailant in the garage a short while ago. I showed him the drawing of Therese Ballard, but he was unable to identify her.

"Tell me about Georges Hervé," I asked. "What was he?"

"An international financier of—how do you say in America? enormous clout. He was a genius, not only in the sheer money market, but also in putting together industrial complexes. He could bring the various parties together in a business marriage, obtain the money from diverse sources, and harmonize the whole project. We knew him because he frequently worked through our Swiss banks. I would say he started to come into real financial power after the war, and he managed to make quite a bit of money during all those years of the unstable French economy. He was anti-Communist, but he was also fiercely opposed to de Gaulle. It is rumored that he contributed quite a bit of money to help defeat the referendum on which de Gaulle's government fell. He was also, of course, opposed to Pompidou, but when d'Estaing came to power, Hervé was once again in favor with the incumbent government."

"But why would anyone want him killed?"

Stefan shrugged. "The French are strange people. Revenge, perhaps. There are still many fanatical Gaullists in France, and they do not forget easily. Or, perhaps someone was trying to destroy his present business negotiations."

"What were his present business negotiations, Stefan?"

"We wish we knew," he said, sipping his Dubonnet. "When a Georges Hervé begins to operate, the whole international community is interested in finding out what is going on. But, alas, there are only rumors."

"Give me the best rumor."

"Let me tell you what I know, and then what I don't know. You must be aware that Hervé did not appear in public much. He worked quietly and facelessly behind the scenes. But, during the past six or eight months, he has been reported to have appeared quite openly in a number of places around Europe."

"Where?"

"West Germany, England, Switzerland, and I also believe in Italy."

"Why, Stefan?"

"That is where the rumors begin. Why was Georges Hervé moving around so openly, almost so desperately? There were so many rumors, but last spring when I was home in Switzerland, one of our leading bankers told me, confidentially, that he had learned that Hervé was organizing an international cartel to produce atomic power for commercial use. Apparently Hervé had found some way to produce atomic energy inexpensively. And the cost factor of atomic energy has been the problem, as you know, Brian. But Hervé's scheme would solve our energy crisis. My banker friend told me that he heard Hervé has been working with a number of private firms in France, Germany, England, and the United States. A private venture, but one which would provide an answer to the energy crisis, and could possibly change the economy of the Western World. Needless to say, it would not be a venture which would please the Arab states or the Communist-bloc nations."

I thought about it for a moment, and then I asked Stefan: "How much credence do you put in that particular rumor?"

"Ah, Brian, you should never put too much credence in any rumor. Let me say, though, that my banker friend in Switzerland is usually correct. But he is sometimes wrong. So it must remain just that—a rumor. However, it is the best rumor I know at the moment."

"Well, I thank you for it, Stefan."

"Tell me, Brian, what are you going to do with this dubious piece of information I gave you?"

"I don't know. I hope it will lead me to Hervé's killers."

Stefan frowned. "A word of advice, Brian. Whoever killed Georges Hervé—whether they are Gaullists or Communists—they are evidently organized and ruthless people. And dangerous. Why would you want to get any further involved in this perilous business?"

"Why not? What have I got to lose?"

Stefan looked at me intently for a moment, as if he were remembering all the events of these recent years. "Yes," he said softly. "I understand."

CHAPTER NINE

Annie had departed the office for the day when I returned, but she left me a note that Tom Ferris had called twice.

I placed a call to Tom, and he said he had something for me and would be right over. When he entered the office, he threw a number of copies of a line drawing of a man's face on my desk.

"That's Therese Ballard's friend at Henri's restaurant."

I studied the drawing of a fat-faced man with thick, set lips. The hair was plastered straight back, and he seemed to be somewhere in middle age.

"I don't know how good that is," Tom said, "because we only had Henri's recollections to rely on. Last evening we had both you and Annie to do the reconstruction of the Ballard woman. However, Henri seemed fairly satisfied when he finished with the artist I brought over there. And you might couple that with the verbal description Henri gave me—heavy-set man, early fifties, full face, thick lips, about five-seven, around 190 pounds. And probably middle European."

"I wonder where he is now?"

"I don't know, but I think I know the whereabouts of Therese Ballard—or whatever the hell her name is."

I sat upright in my chair. "Shoot."

Tom flicked open his notepad. "I engaged Andy Cohen's firm up in New York to work on this, and they're an excellent organization. They took those Ballard pictures out to JFK and began circulating them around the airline clerks. Nothing showed up on the morning flights, but they found out that a delayed TWA flight left for Paris shortly after midnight last night. One of Andy's boys found the airline clerk at home, and when she saw our picture, she made a positive identification. It seems that flight had been delayed for four or five hours, but a few minutes before it finally took off, a woman came rushing up to the counter saying she had a reservation on a flight today but she had just learned of the delayed flight and could she get on. And there was space available. The agent said she had dark hair, but she was sure it was a wig and it was the same woman in our drawing."

"That could be right. If they jumped me about six thirty, they could have driven directly to New York in that time. Exceptionally fast driving, but not too difficult. And they were in luck again. A delayed flight and she stepped right on. Was she alone?"

"All by herself. Very little luggage. Andy's men went back to the TWA desk and got the passenger's name and passport number. Marie Delacroix. And here's the French passport number." He tore a page from his notebook and handed a slip of paper to me. "But I wouldn't count too heavily on that. I'll bet it's a forged passport."

"It probably is, but I'll check it out."

"So your little bird has flown away to Paris. What do we do now?"

"I don't know. We just have to find her somehow."

I was thinking of telling Tom about my encounter and the killing in the garage earlier today. But I dismissed that idea. Tom might get scrupulous about something like that and feel he would have to report it to the police. Furthermore, it was my fight, not Tom's.

After Tom left I sat there for some time, studying the drawings of Ballard and her friend. The phone rang, and when

I answered it, Jacques Duval came on the line, his voice extremely agitated.

"Brian, I have to see you right away," he said. "There has been the most extraordinary development in this whole affair."

I told him to come right over to my office, and I was thinking that from the sound of his voice maybe somebody at the embassy had been able to identify the drawing of Therese Ballard. Maybe we were getting lucky for a change.

When Duval entered my office twenty minutes later, his face was flushed and he was mopping perspiration off his brow. I held up the drawing of Therese Ballard, and asked him: "Have you identified the woman?"

He looked at me in bewilderment, as if he couldn't quite understand my question, and then he shook his head. "No, no we do not know who she is. But, *merde,* something unbelievable has happened, and the ambassador wants me to ask you a question."

He was breathing heavily and there was a bewildered expression on his face. I told him to sit down and tell me about it calmly.

"The ambassador just received a call on the wireless from Paris," he said. "He was told that the body of Georges Hervé arrived there in the early evening, Paris time. Some of the family was there to meet it, and one of them had to identify it. And *alors,* it is not the body of Georges Hervé."

I was prepared for a lot of things but not for that, and silence filled my office as I allowed the ramifications of this incredible twist to set in.

Finally, I asked Duval: "The identification was absolutely sure?"

"Absolutely. His own daughter. Then they brought in one of the member's of Hervé's firm to see if he could identify the body. He couldn't. And then they took fingerprints from the corpse."

"And?"

"They couldn't trace them immediately. Of course, it is late evening in Paris now, and they have not had time to do a completely thorough fingerprint search through the files as yet. They will do that tomorrow. But a preliminary fingerprint check revealed nothing. But, for the moment, they have an unidentified corpse on their hands who was supposed to be Monsieur Hervé."

"Damn," I said.

"Brian, I am telling you this because the ambassador wants me to ask you a question. This man—this unknown corpse—in Paris, are you sure it is the same man who arrived from Paris two days ago representing himself as Hervé?"

"Certain. I had Tom Ferris's men pick him up at the airport, and they kept him in constant surveillance until they passed him over to me the night he was killed. There was no chance of a switch after he got off that Air France plane. The switch took place someplace earlier."

"You mentioned that there was a last-minute change of plans, that Hervé was originally due to arrive the preceding day. Is there any possibility that he actually did, and then this imposter arrived the following day?"

"Not a chance. Ferris's men were watching that flight, too. They would have spotted Hervé, even if he were disguised. No, Hervé never reached Washington. An imposter came in his place."

"Ah, but why? Paris told the ambassador this afternoon that the corpse bears some resemblance to the real Hervé, but there are many discrepancies. The body is small and dark, yes, and it has a mustache, but the real Hervé's face is rather sharp and angular, while the imposter's is slightly plump. And also the real Hervé's hair is quite thin on top, and this man's was full."

"And nobody caught that before the body was shipped back to Paris?"

"I was the only one from the embassy staff to see the body, but I have never met Hervé before. I just assumed it was he. Of course, the ambassador knew Hervé, but he did not attend the autopsy."

"And the fellow we were going to visit in Chevy Chase, Metivier, he had never met him before, either. Thus, for almost eighteen hours after the murder, nobody who ever knew Hervé actually saw the body. And meanwhile we were all running around in circles, chasing the wrong trail. Maybe that's the way they set it up for us."

"But where is the real Hervé, Brian?"

"It could be a kidnaping, but I don't think so. Apparently there's been no kidnap note, and in a kidnaping you don't have an imposter take the place of the victim. Of course, Hervé himself, for some strange reason, could have switched places with the man who was killed. Maybe he knew he was in danger of being hit, and he had this guy act as a stand-in for him. But I tend to discount that. It sounds as if Hervé has been abducted. Maybe they're holding him someplace, trying to pry information out of him, and maybe that's why the imposter was used—to give them time to work Hervé over before people started looking for him. Or, maybe Hervé has already been killed."

"*Sacrebleu!*"

"You need a drink, Jacques," I said, and I went over to my file cabinet and pulled out a bottle of brandy I keep stashed there. While he took a deep draught of the brandy, I tried to sort it out in my mind. There were dozens of questions. Who was the dead imposter we had shipped back to Paris? When was the switch made? Why was the switch made? And where the hell was Hervé now?

But the most important unanswered question revolved around the murder last night. Did the Ballard people realize they were killing an imposter? Or, did they think they were killing the real Hervé? And, as a corollary to that, was the imposter who was killed last night carrying the authentic papers everyone wants so much?

I knew now that I couldn't get the answer to these questions in Washington. I would have to start at the beginning of the trail where the real Hervé was last seen and then pick it up from there. Paris. Of course, there was an even more urgent reason for wanting to go to Paris now. That's where Therese Ballard had flown last night. If I could find Hervé, I might very well be able to find Therese Ballard. Their paths apparently crossed at some juncture.

I looked across the desk at Duval. I still didn't completely trust him, but I needed some assistance from him now. I decided to bring him into my confidence a little bit. I didn't tell him about the drawing we had obtained of the man who was Ballard's friend, but I did tell him about Ballard's flight from JFK last night. I gave him the name and passport number she had used, and asked him if he would check it out for me. He agreed.

"Then, Jacques, I need some assistance in Paris. I'm flying over there and chase this thing down."

"When?"

I picked up the phone, and dialed Air France, and in a few minutes I had a reservation on a flight leaving Dulles for Paris at nine o'clock that evening.

"Do you know who would be in charge of the Hervé investigation in Paris?" I asked Duval.

"No, but I am sure it will be somebody of rank. Here, let me give you the name of a senior police official at the Sûreté, Inspector Croteau. He will most surely be involved in this." He took out a small pad, and with a thin gold pencil, he rapidly began to write some names on it. "I am giving you Croteau's name, and also the names of some people in the foreign office who might be able to help you. I will cable all these people this evening, and ask them to offer you any help or courtesy you need. I will also ask Croteau to get that information about the passport for you."

Duval looked more composed, now that there was something positive he could do. But I wanted to get moving, and I wanted him to leave. I took the slip of paper from him, and rose from behind the desk. "Thanks, Jacques."

"Brian, it has been a most perplexing experience for all of us. The ambassador and all of us would be most grateful for whatever you could do to untangle it."

"I'll see what I can dig up in Paris."

"*Bonne chance.*"

"I don't like that phrase, Jacques. That's the one Therese Ballard used when I last saw her."

I drove home to get my passport and threw a few things in a bag for the trip to Paris. Actually, I only packed a small suitcase because this was hardly going to be a vacation trip. However, I had some problems about what to do with my pistol. I couldn't very well carry it on board the airplane in my holster because it would surely be picked up by all the anti-hijacking security devices. I would have to hide it in my bag, and just hope that the French customs in Paris would not confiscate it when I passed through.

Then, holding the .32 in my hand, I suddenly decided to take a heavier weapon to Paris with me. I went in to that trunk I have bolted to the floor in my utility room, unlocked it, and extracted a .38 revolver. It was the old reliable Smith and Wesson .38, the Military and Police Special used by law-enforcement agencies throughout the world. A thirty-ounce weapon holding six cartridges, it was a heftier pistol than the .32 and it had more range. I also decided to take along a shoulder holster, and two boxes of extra cartridges.

By pushing and shoving, I managed to get the pistol and the cartridges in my shaving kit, and I was trying to figure out where to put it in my suitcase when I finally decided to keep it out of the suitcase until the last minute before I had to surrender my bag at the check-in counter.

It was a most fortunate decision.

I called Annie before I left for the airport, telling her I would be gone for an indefinite period, then phoned Tom Ferris and told him about the unidentified corpse that had been flown back to Paris. Tom whistled, and then I told him I was leaving for Paris in a few hours.

"What do you expect to find over there?" he asked.

"Therese Ballard. And a lot of answers."

It was shortly after seven when I left my house. I threw the suitcase in the back seat, but I kept the shaving kit with the pistol inside it on the seat beside me. I was going to take the George Washington Parkway out toward Dulles, but when I pulled away from my house, I decided to save some time in getting to the parkway by cutting through an industrial-commercial area behind Route 1. It's a busy place during the daytime but now, after business hours, there would be no traffic and I could pick up some time.

I was about a half-mile from my house when I noticed the car following behind me. A large, dark Buick. And now it was drawing up on me. Was it a tail? I had only noticed the car behind me a few minutes ago, but it could very well have been parked near my house and then come after me when I pulled away. As the car drew nearer, I could see that there were two men in the front seat.

I was just at the beginning of the industrial-commercial area now and I decided that, if it were a tail, this was a good place to lose it. The warehouses and the plants were all closed, and there was no traffic and nobody on the street. As I came around the corner, I gunned the engine of my Olds and took off down that deserted street. But at the very same instant the Buick behind me gunned its engine, and came screaming around the corner after me.

That Buick had some kind of incredibly souped-up engine, and it moved right up on me, almost as if I were driving in slow motion.

It was only a few yards behind me when I spotted a side street, a narrow lane running between two rows of commercial buildings. If I could make a quick and unexpected turn, I might catch the Buick by surprise, and it would go racing past the side street before it had an opportunity to turn after me. I waited until the last second, and then I twisted the steering wheel furiously to the right, aiming for that side street.

I made the turn, almost on two wheels, and for a moment I thought I had lost the Buick. But somehow the Buick, traveling at those amazingly fast speeds, was able to negotiate a turn. I had to brake to pull out of my turn, and that gave the Buick the opportunity it wanted. As I came around in an arc, the Buick instead took the turn on a diagonal line.

And now it was heading straight for me, trying to ram me.

It hit me somewhere near my rear door, and my Olds spun around in a dizzy circle. I was trying to fight for control, and brake the car to a stop, but I went up over a curb and slammed into a brick wall. Fortunately, I had braked the car to slow speed, but there was still a hell of a crash when it hit the wall. I was dazed, but uninjured.

And then the bullets started coming.

The Buick was about twenty-five yards away, stopped in the middle of the street, and the two men were climbing out. The one in the passenger seat had an automatic rifle in his hands, and he was pumping shots off at my car. The first ones hit the side window, smashing through and leaving a gaping hole. I knew from the size of that hole and the loud report of the rifle that he was using magnum shells. I had to get out of that car, because magnum shells can rip through the metal of an automobile.

Grabbing my shaving kit from the front seat, I slid out of the car, and went into a low crouch, running toward a doorway a few feet away. I was almost at the doorway when I felt a sharp sting in my arm above the left elbow, and I knew I had been hit. I got to the doorway, and tried the door, but it was locked. However, the doorway was recessed, and I leaned up against a brick wall and pulled the .38 out of the shaving kit.

The two of them were now both coming cautiously toward me, and they were coming from different angles. The guy with the rifle was coming from my left, and the driver of the car, who now had a pistol in his hand, was coming from the right. The one I was most fearful of was the fellow with the rifle—he looked like he had a Remington, and that meant he probably could have as many as twenty of those deadly seven-mm shells in there.

I fired a shot from my .38, without taking careful aim, just enough to stop him from moving in on me. I missed, of course, but he went down on one knee and brought the rifle up to eye level. And then, a shot rang out from the fellow with the pistol to my right. It hit about two feet above me on the brick of the alcove where I was standing. And I knew then that he had magnum bullets, too, and he was probably firing a .357 magnum revolver.

I fired a shot in his direction, and he started returning fire rapidly. He shouted something to the fellow with the rifle, and at that moment the rifleman rose to his feet and started a charge at me. It was to be a diversionary tactic—the fellow with the pistol would keep me pinned down while the rifleman made his rush at me.

I didn't buy it.

I pulled back behind the brick of the doorway, waited a few seconds, and then reached around to the direction from where the rifleman would be coming. He was about ten feet away, running straight for the doorway, his rifle on his hip. I fired and the first shot missed, but the second one hit him squarely in the chest.

He took one more step, an anguished expression on his face, and then he pitched forward, hitting the ground with dead weight, as the rifle clattered away.

Then I fired once more at the fellow with the handgun, and I reached down into my shaving kit, which was lying on the ground, to get another box of cartridges and I noticed the blood running down over my left hand. The handgun out there had seen his companion go down, and he now became more cautious. He ducked behind a parked car. I took the opportunity to move out of the doorway and get over behind my car. He saw the move, and fired a shot at me, but he missed.

Then I saw him start to run. He was trying to get back to his car, but it was too far away and it meant he would have to run in exposed space where I could nip him. He ran behind a parked delivery truck, and I fired at him, but I don't think I got him. I came out from behind my car in a low crouch, and I dashed over toward that delivery truck, leaning up against it. He was on the other side. But then I realized I had fired six shots, and my pistol was empty. However, I still had that box of shells in my left hand.

I swung out the cylinder of the .38, tapped it, and rapidly started pushing cartridges into it. I didn't have time to load it fully, but I did manage to get three bullets into the chamber before I swung the cylinder shut. There was no noise from the other side of the delivery truck, and I didn't know if he was aware I was on the other side. There was a low railing on the roof of the truck for carrying luggage up there, and I quietly reached up and grabbed it and pulled myself up on the roof. Lying flat on my stomach, I inched over to the other edge and peered down.

The fellow with the handgun was crouched near the front fender, carefully looking around it to see where I was. I pulled the trigger twice, and I think both bullets got him. However, the first shot alone would have done it—the bullet, coming from above, entered his head just behind the ear. He spun around, and fell over on his back.

The whole scene had taken place in an incredibly short time, and nobody had appeared yet to investigate the sound of all the shots. I jumped down from the top of the truck, and ran toward my car. I wanted to get out of there immediately before the cops showed up, and I hoped my car would work. Both front fenders were smashed in and the lights were broken, but the engine was still running when I reached the Olds. There was some grating and scraping as I tried to drive it off the sidewalk and back onto the street, but it went.

I spun the wheel immediately, gunned the engine, and got the hell out of there. I didn't even bother to look back at my two friends lying on the street—I was sure they were both dead.

I kept driving at high speeds until I got on the George Washington Parkway, looking back in my rear-view mirror constantly to see if anyone else was trailing me. I didn't stop until sometime later when I was on the Dulles Access Road. There was practically no traffic out there, and so I pulled over to the side to inspect my wound. I slipped off my jacket, and rolled up my sleeve, and saw that I had taken a flesh wound in the arm above the elbow. There was a lot of blood, but the wound wasn't serious. I wiped off some of the blood with a handkerchief, and then tied the handkerchief around the wound to stop the bleeding. I was fortunate, I felt, because if that magnum shell had been an inch closer on target it would have really smashed up my arm.

The two gunmen back there had obviously been sent by the Ballard people. They must have been staked out somewhere near my house, and their instructions were quite definite. If the man in the garage this morning had been sent to warn me off, then these two had been sent to finish me off. There would be no more warnings. I was coming after them, and I was apparently making them extremely apprehensive. And they wanted me stopped.

There was no use, I felt, in hanging around and trying to do some research on the two men I had just killed. Like the man this morning, they were probably local guns hired for this one job, and I wouldn't be able to find any strong link between them and the Ballard people. Furthermore, if I had to answer a lot of questions to the police, it would only delay me. And I had immediate business in Paris.

The Air France 727 took off shortly after nine o'clock and I rested my head back on the seat and closed my eyes. The plane was fairly crowded, but there were only a few people in my first-class section and I was grateful for that. A few minutes later, a hostess came by and served drinks, but when she brought my dinner I only fiddled with it. After she had taken the tray away, I turned off the overhead light, and closed my eyes again, falling into a deep sleep.

When I awakened it was morning, and the hostess was standing beside me, offering a cup of *café noir.* I had only taken a few sips when the captain announced over the intercom that we were making our descent toward the new Charles de Gaulle Airport outside Paris. I looked out in the distance, and I could see Paris, with the Eiffel Tower jutting high into the air.

I wondered where Therese Ballard was down there. And I also wondered if Georges Hervé was down there. I was now beginning to have some second thoughts about our friend Hervé. I didn't know the man, of course, but everyone seemed to say he was astute and crafty, an adroit manipulator of situations. Could he have possibly engineered the switch between himself and the man who was killed in Chevy Chase? Was he the mastermind of the whole thing? Or, was he simply a victim? Was he being held in captivity someplace down there in Paris? Was he even alive?

The captain told us to fasten our seat belts.

CHAPTER TEN

It was shortly after nine in the morning, Paris time, when I passed through the passport-control gate.

I had no trouble with the customs people. When they asked if I had anything to declare, I said no. And, when I told them I was a tourist, they didn't even bother to open my suitcase with the .38 in it. They merely stamped it and let me go through.

I hailed a taxi outside the airport and settled back in the cab for the ride into the city. There were a number of trucks on the road, and we passed a horse-drawn wagon loaded with hay, its driver perched imperturbably on the dray seat, French peasant cap pulled low on his forehead, a pipe clenched between his teeth. The traffic increased as we reached the outskirts of Paris, the early-morning flow of a city starting the new business day—some delivery trucks, the rush of commuters, and a bevy of those small European cars that darted in and out of lanes with astonishing velocity. I directed the driver to take me to a small hotel where I usually stayed on the Boulevard Malesherbes near the Madeleine. It was inexpensive, centrally located, and did not cater to the American tourist crowd. The clerk behind the desk recognized me immediately, his face breaking into a broad grin, but he frowned when I told him I needed a room. Ah, but why did not Monsieur Petersen let us know he was coming? There are no reservations available. Monsieur Petersen did not know he was coming until last evening. An emergency trip. The desk clerk thought for a moment, and then the grin returned. He would find a room for me, a good one. Some Germans were scheduled to check in later this morning (he said the word German with evident disdain), and he would juggle things around and give them some other room.

My room faced the boulevard and it had a small balcony, and while I was showering and shaving, the desk clerk sent up a continental breakfast, which I ate on the balcony after I had changed into fresh clothing. Sipping my coffee, I watched the street scene below me, and memories of other days in Paris came flooding in on me. I sat there awhile, caught in my reverie, thinking of how life had been for me in that halcyon time, and then—inevitably—my mind moved forward in recollection, and I began to think of Marge. But I broke that off, and drained the last of my coffee. On the sidewalk across the boulevard, two young French girls in their early twenties were walking along, talking animatedly, and I watched them, their firm young bodies moving gracefully beneath their sheath dresses, until they disappeared around a corner at the end of the block.

A short while later I went down to the boulevard and hailed a cab, directing the driver to take me over to the Sûreté. The taxi drove down the Rue Royal and then circled around the Place de la Concorde, and I had a chance to glance up the Champs Elysées toward the Arc de Triomphe, always an impressive sight for me, then along the quay that ran beside the Seine, until we came to the Ile de Saint Louis in the middle of the river. The driver made a right-hand turn onto one of the small bridges, the Pont Marie and a few seconds later pulled up in front of the Sûreté, that old bastion of Paris law enforcement. Inside the building I inquired for Inspector Croteau, the name Duval had given me in Washington, and without much delay I was directed to an office on the second floor, where I was greeted by a thin, middle-aged man with a tired-looking face. He was wearing steel-rimmed glasses, and he took them off when I entered the office, as if to obtain a better look at me. He rose, shook my hand, and directed me to a wooden chair opposite his desk. The office was old, and had a musty smell about it, and the inspector's desk was littered with papers.

"I have been expecting your arrival, Monsieur Petersen," he said, "but not quite so soon. You Americans are very swift." He spoke in a slow, measured French, but his gray eyes were sharp and alert, and fastened intently upon me.

I made some comment about wanting to follow this thing up as soon as possible, and I asked him if they had been able to identify the body of Hervé's imposter yet.

He shook his head slowly and reached for some papers on the desk. "The fingerprints have not been identified at this moment, but we are still working on it. I am also turning the prints over to Interpol today. They may come up with something."

"And no information as to the whereabouts of Georges Hervé?"

He shook his head again, slowly, still regarding me carefully. "And your interest in this, Monsieur Petersen?"

"I was with the supposed Hervé when he was killed in Washington."

"Ah, yes, I have a confidential memorandum from the foreign office about that," he said, reaching for another piece of paper. He studied it for a second, his lips pursed. "And now you want to find the murderers? Revenge, perhaps?"

I knew where his suspicions were leading him, and I deliberately allowed him to be carried along. "Something like that," I said.

"Your business in the United States, Monsieur Petersen?"

"Public relations."

"Ah, yes." He was thinking, of course, that I was perhaps an agent of the CIA, a normal suspicion, and I was happy to allow him to entertain it. The Europeans were almost morbidly suspicious of CIA activities today, and when some unexplained American like myself starts rooting around in a police affair, their fears are naturally aroused. And there was no way for him to check it out. If he asked me bluntly if I were CIA, I would naturally deny it, even if I were. And neither the CIA itself, nor the American Government, would confirm it if I were. Inspector Croteau remained silent for a moment, and I could almost see his mental processes at work. He wasn't necessarily convinced that I was CIA, but he was going to work on the assumption that I was.

"The foreign office has asked us to cooperate with you," he said. "And, naturally, we shall."

"I appreciate that, Inspector."

"This memo from the foreign office," he said, handing it to me. "It is correct?"

I scanned the memo, and saw it was substantially the same story I had told Duval in Washington. "It is correct," I said. "How much public notice of this affair has there been in Paris?"

"None at all. None of the international wire services apparently picked up the first story of the attack on the presumed Hervé in Washington, and the family of Monsieur Hervé did not want to announce the death until after the body had been returned and funeral arrangements had been made. By that time, of course, we knew that Monsieur Hervé had not been killed—at least not in Washington."

"And that story was not released to the press?"

Croteau paused. "The office of the Minister of Internal Affairs thought that it would not be ... opportune to release it at this time. We still do not know what has happened. And, of course, the police are very happy to cooperate in that decision.

It will make our work that much easier. We are conducting a regular investigation for the disappearance of Georges Hervé. Until we know something more, we shall not say anything to the press. Hervé's family prefers it that way, and so does his business firm." He accepted the memo I handed back to him. "And, naturally, this is a completely confidential memo," he said.

I took out of my pocket the two drawings the artist had done in Washington, the one of the Ballard woman and the one of the heavy-set man. "These are the people mentioned in that report," I said. "Recognize either of them?"

He adjusted his glasses and peered at both pictures. He put down the Ballard picture, shaking his head, but he held the other one in his hand, still looking at it. "There is a resemblance," he said slowly. "Perhaps...."

"You recognize it?"

"It bears a faint resemblance to...." His voice trailed off. "Would you excuse me for a moment, Monsieur Petersen? I would like to discuss this with someone else."

He left the office, and I remained there alone for almost fifteen minutes. Croteau returned with the picture still in his hand. "May we keep this?" he asked.

I nodded yes, and said: "A possible identification?"

"Perhaps. The eyes and the ears are not right, but it does resemble Alexander Hartel."

"Alexander Hartel?"

"A Hungarian. A very clever and a very ruthless man. He works for causes ... sympathetic to the Iron Curtain countries. Even now we are looking for him to question him about an incident which happened here in Paris last year. We would very much like to question Monsieur Hartel. If Hartel is involved in this...." he said, his voice trailing off again. "I thank you for this information, Monsieur Petersen. It is most valuable. I shall pass it along to Interpol."

"And your own investigation of Hervé's disappearance, Inspector? Have you discovered anything yet?"

He spread his hands out. "We have done all the usual things. If Monsieur Hervé has disappeared, we must first look for him in his familiar habitats. He has a home at St. Tropez. But he is not there. Nor is he at his other home in Normandy. We traced his activities on the day of his departure. He left his villa at Fontainebleau, went to his office in Paris, and his secretary, a Paul Bremmond, drove him to the airport. That was the last he was seen. We checked all the other flights on that day, but he was not listed."

"And so the switch was made at the airport?"

"Presumably."

"Then who is the other man?"

"We shall find out—eventually. There is not much to work on at the moment. A small overnight bag was returned with the body, but it revealed nothing. Shirts, underclothes, things like that, all purchased here in Paris. The suit he was wearing, however, was made in England. But that is not unusual. Many Frenchmen are today buying the English woolens. Nevertheless, I have sent a set of fingerprints, plus a photograph of the corpse, to Scotland Yard. I must explore every avenue."

"Do you have any hypotheses you're working on, Inspector?"

"Hypotheses are an extremely dangerous thing in a police investigation, Monsieur Petersen. They force the mind into a set pattern, and you are not free for new ideas. However … there are many possibilities, and we shall investigate them all. First, perhaps Monsieur Hervé was abducted at the airport—not as difficult a thing to do as you might imagine. And then, the unidentified man was substituted for him. Ah, but then he was killed in America. Did the killers know it was not the real Monsieur Hervé? More interesting possibilities there. If they did not know it was the real Hervé, there is the possibility of more people involved. Or, if they knew it was not Hervé, then maybe they wanted to kill their own man—perhaps because he knew too much. That still leaves the question as to the present location of Monsieur Hervé. Alive, or dead? A second major possibility is that Hervé himself might have arranged the substitution...."

"For what reason?"

"Innumerable reasons. Perhaps—and a Parisian would think of this—it is an affair of the heart, and Hervé wanted to steal away to some secret liaison for awhile, with someone else taking his place. And, mistakenly, the substitute is killed." Inspector Croteau paused, reflecting on his own words. "But that is not a very serious possibility. There are stronger ones. Suppose that Hervé is in serious financial difficulties, and he wants it to appear as if he has been killed. Insurance money, or a new beginning somewhere else. We are investigating Monsieur Hervé's financial status very carefully."

"But Hervé would have known that the body couldn't be passed off as his."

"Perhaps something went wrong. Maybe there was more to the plan than we know, and it did not work out perfectly. Some way to represent the corpse as Hervé's body."

"I don't know," I said, uncertainly.

"But now, with the possible entrance of Alexander Hartel into the picture, another alternative opens. Hervé might have tried to plan his own murder, and in collaboration with Hartel he might have fled behind the Iron Curtain. At this very moment, our Monsieur Hervé may be sitting very comfortably in some eastern country."

I smiled. "You don't trust anybody, do you, Inspector?"

"It is not a question of trust, Monsieur Petersen. Merely keeping one's mind open for … possibilities."

"And, of course, you're keeping your mind open on me."

"Of course," he said, brightly, "but I shall cooperate with you, as the foreign office requested."

I asked him about the passport number that Tom Ferris had obtained from JFK Airport in New York, and Croteau said that it was being run through the passport division this morning, and he would inform me about it as soon as he received any information. I also asked him if I could look at the body in the police morgue. I wanted to be sure that one more switch hadn't been pulled.

Croteau himself escorted me down to the morgue, and an attendant took us into a room lined with tiers of lockers built into the walls. The attendant consulted a paper he was holding, then opened one of the doors and pulled out a slab on which a body lay, covered by a white sheet. Croteau removed the sheet from the face, and I saw it was the same man who had been killed on the street in Chevy Chase. He still seemed to have that quizzical expression on his face.

"*Oui?*" Croteau asked.

"*Oui,*" I said.

Croteau walked with me to the front steps of the building, and I inquired of him the address of Hervé's business firm. He gave it to me and also told me that he would telephone there immediately to alert them to my coming and to ask their cooperation. Jules Giroux was the man to see, he said, the executive director of the firm in Hervé's absence. I gave Croteau the address of my hotel, and he said he would be in contact with me as soon as anything further developed.

I shook hands with Croteau and stepped into a waiting cab. As I pulled away, two uniformed *gendarmes* were entering the building, and Croteau said something to them, briefly, then watched my departing cab, his eyes squinting in the bright Parisian sun.

Hervé's office was located in a building on the Rue du 4 Septembre, immediately adjacent to the Bourse, the financial center of Paris. A sign on the door said simply: *Hervé et Cie.* I presented my card to a receptionist, and a few seconds later she told me that Monsieur Giroux would see me immediately. A heavy paneled door opened, and Jules Giroux came out to escort me into his office. He was probably somewhere in his late forties, a medium-sized man with thinning hair. He wore a dark business suit with a vest, and a thin golden chain protruded from a fob pocket. His office was decorated in Empire style, a mahogany table instead of a desk, thick carpeting on the floor, and a small oil painting on the far wall.

"Inspector Croteau from the Sûreté has just called me about your visit," he said, offering me a chair. He spoke quietly, but there was a touch of apprehension in his voice. "We are most distressed about Monsieur Hervé's disappearance."

"So am I."

"You are investigating this for the American Government?" Giroux asked.

"Let's just say that I'm an American who's investigating this."

"I understand," Giroux said, and I wondered what he understood.

"You've had no contact with Monsieur Hervé since he disappeared the other day?" I asked.

"Not a word, and we are *most* concerned."

"Did Monsieur Hervé often go away on business trips?"

"Rather frequently, and much more frequently in the past year. But we usually knew where he was going. Or, sometimes he would send us telegrams, in a business code we use. His absence would not distress me at all right now, if it were not for that inexplicable tragedy in the United States. We received notice that Monsier Hervé had been killed, and then … well, of course, you know. The body was not his. But we have no idea of what happened to poor Monsieur Hervé. And now, this morning …" He put his hand to his forehead. "A reporter from *Le Figaro* phoned me. It seems that one of their people was checking through a Washington newspaper and saw the notice of a Georges Hervé who was killed, and this reporter wanted to know if that was our Monsieur Hervé. I told him that of course it wasn't, which was true. But then the reporter wanted to know where Monsieur Hervé was at the moment. I had to invent some story about his being on vacation on the Riviera, but I do not know if I convinced the reporter. *Hélas,* we would not want this to appear in the press. It would be most disadvantageous for our business."

"Yeah, your business," I commented dryly. "Are you sure that Monsieur Hervé actually went to the airport on the fifteenth?"

"Positive. Let me call Monsieur Bremmond in here. He is Monsieur Hervé's private secretary, and he drove him to the airport." Giroux spoke into an intercom, and a few seconds later a young man in his early thirties came into the office. He, too, was dressed in a conservative business suit, but he was trim and handsome and had a full head of dark black hair. Giroux introduced us, and then he said to the secretary: "Paul, this gentleman wants to be sure that you actually took Monsieur Hervé to the airport on the fifteenth."

"Of course. I drove him there in my own car."

"Did you go into the terminal building with him?" I asked.

"No, I merely left him at the passenger entrance and then drove back here to the office."

"What kind of luggage was Monsieur Hervé carrying?"

The secretary sat down and thought for a moment. He did not seem to mind the interrogation, and there was a look of mystification in his eyes. "Let me see," he said. "A briefcase, of course. And a brown valise. A large one, in which you could perhaps put two suits."

I recalled that Hervé's imposter had only been carrying a small black overnight bag. That meant that, at least, Hervé and his impostor had not switched luggage, or had it switched for them.

"Are you aware," I asked, "that Hervé was originally scheduled to arrive in America on the fourteenth?"

"Yes," the secretary, Bremmond, said. "At the last moment, on the very day that he was scheduled to leave, he changed reservations."

"Did he often do that?"

"No ..." Bremmond said, slowly. "But ..."

"But what?" I insisted.

Bremmond glanced at Giroux, and I wondered what that look meant. "Monsieur Hervé has been doing things quite unusually of late."

"What do you mean?"

Bremmond looked at Giroux again, and Giroux shrugged his shoulders. "Go on, tell him, Paul," he said.

"Both Monsieur Giroux and myself are usually Monsieur Hervé's confidants in all the firm's business negotiations, but during the last few months he has become very secretive about all his operations——"

"Or, at least about the big operation, Paul," interrupted Giroux.

"Yes, the big operation," Bremmond corrected himself. "The firm has been engaged in attempting to conclude an extremely large business venture, and while Monsieur Giroux and myself were most intimately engaged in the opening stages of it, we have been excluded from everything for the last number of months. Monsieur Hervé refused to discuss it with us. He did all his own correspondence on the matter, and all his own telephone negotiations."

"And he never did that before?" I asked.

"Never."

"Would there be anyone else in the firm whom he would take into his confidence?"

"No one," Giroux answered, sharply. "Paul is his private, confidential secretary, and I am the executive director of the firm."

"What was the nature of this large venture?" I asked.

"Oh, Monsieur Petersen, I could not tell you that," Giroux said. "Monsieur Hervé would be most displeased."

"For God's sake, Hervé may be dead, for all we know."

Giroux rubbed his hand over his forehead. "I cannot even contemplate that possibility," he said.

I continued to probe away at the question of Hervé's business interest to see if I could verify the rumor that Stefan Meyner had told me in Washington, but I wasn't able to dislodge any more information from the two men. We talked for another fifteen minutes about the disappearance, but nothing new was unearthed. Finally, I asked if it would be possible for me to visit Hervé's family.

"The police interrogated them quite thoroughly yesterday," Bremmond said. "But … I suppose, if you want …"

"I do want to," I said.

"They are probably resting today, after that ordeal of yesterday. I accompanied Celine—Mademoiselle Hervé, that is, the daughter—to the morgue for that horrible scene. But I will phone her. Perhaps tomorrow."

"I'd appreciate that."

"I will give you their address in Fontainebleau," Bremmond said, and he scratched it on a piece of paper that he handed to me.

I thanked them both for their cooperation, and Bremmond escorted me to the outer office. I asked him one last question: "Did Hervé tell you the reason for changing his flight plans at the last moment?"

"No," he said, shaking his head. "He never told me anything recently. But at one time...." There was sadness in the young man's voice.

That afternoon I visited the offices of *Le Monde* and asked if I could do some research in their newspaper file. I told them that I was a professor of modem European history and that I wanted to look up some recent data. I rummaged around in the "H" file, but I only found a few clippings about Georges Hervé, all of them small notices from the business section about various mergers and acquisitions that involved his firm. Nothing there. Later, I walked over to my old Army Intelligence office on the *Rue Royale*, hoping I could find somebody from the old days who might give me some help, but there had been a complete change-over of staff and there was no one in the office whom I knew. The passage of time.

When I arrived back at my hotel, there was a note for me in my mailbox. A short letter from Inspector Croteau, written in a precise hand on the Sûreté stationery, and delivered by messenger. It said, tersely, that the passport number that we had obtained for the Ballard woman's departure from New York was a forgery. Croteau also stated that Scotland Yard had not been able to identify the fingerprints of the corpse at the Paris police station.

More dead ends.

I was tired after the flight across the Atlantic, with the resultant metabolism changes, and so I decided to have an early dinner someplace and then retire. Tomorrow I could try my luck at Fontainebleau.

CHAPTER ELEVEN

I rented a small Citroen in the morning and drove the sixty kilometers south to Fontainebleau.

The day was warm, and after I had passed through the suburbs of Paris with all those dreadful new American-style apartment buildings, I welcomed the fresh country air rushing through my window. I had obtained a map from the car-rental agency that directed me along the new *autoroute,* enabling me to reach Fontainebleau in about an hour. The Hervé residence was actually a manor estate located on the eastern side of the old city, and I had to ask directions a number of times before I could find it. A long, sweeping driveway led up to a stately, red-brick mansion, and when I parked the car, there was not a sound to be heard.

I pushed a bell on the side of a wrought-iron doorway that was backed by glass panes, and a few seconds later it was opened by a fat woman in a black maid's uniform. I told her I would like to see Madame Hervé, gave her my card and told her that I thought I was expected. She ushered me into a paneled drawing room, and I waited there alone for almost fifteen minutes, inspecting the oil paintings on the wall. One of them looked like an original Matisse.

A footstep behind, and I turned to see a young woman in her early twenties. Her black hair was brushed back from a broad, candid face, and she was wearing a simple cotton dress and leather sandals. She approached me, extending her hand in the French custom, and we shook hands.

"I am Celine Hervé," she said. Her voice was soft and pleasant.

I introduced myself and told her I was investigating her father's disappearance.

"Yes, Paul Bremmond telephoned me about you," she said, switching to English.

"I'd like to ask your mother and yourself some questions," I said.

"I do not know what more we can say. We told the police everything yesterday." Her English was quite good, and it had a winsome trace of British accent in it.

"The obvious question is, Do you know what happened to your father?"

"We are mystified," she said, a deep frown on her forehead. "Papa departed on a business trip for the United States. One of the many business trips he takes. He told us he would be back shortly. And then we received that shocking news that he had been killed. Which, of course, was not true. But what happened?"

"That's what a lot of people would like to find out. Did he tell you where he could be contacted during this trip?"

"No," she said, slowly. "His office usually knows where he is, though."

"But they don't this time."

"That is very strange."

"Is there any chance, Mademoiselle, that your father could have told your mother something more about this trip?"

She shook her head no emphatically. "I am sure my father would have told *me*. We have become very close these last years, Papa and me. Ever since … ever since, my brother."

"Your brother?"

"My older brother, the only other child in the family, was killed during the Algerian War."

"I'm sorry."

"I feel that something quite terrible has happened to Papa, but I can't imagine what." The beginnings of tears were forming in the corners of her eyes. Her anguish appeared sincere, but I was carefully reserving any judgment.

"Would it be possible to speak to your mother?" I asked, softly.

"She is very upset."

"I promise not to upset her any further."

Celine studied my face for a moment. She was about five-six or five-seven, but she still had to look up at me. Finally, she said: "All right, but only for a few minutes."

She led me through the house out toward the gardens in the rear, and I noticed on a table in the corridor a silver-framed photograph. I paused, looking at it. "Is this your father?" I asked. And when she told me that it was, I suddenly realized that this was the first time I had ever seen a picture of the missing Georges Hervé. He was a sharp-faced man with controlled features and intense, flinty eyes, like pieces of granite. He certainly looked more like the international financier than the man who was killed on the street in Chevy Chase.

We found Madame Hervé sitting in a gazebo in the middle of the garden behind the mansion. The gardens were those formal, cultivated gardens the French do so well, with immaculate lawns and finely sculptured bushes and hedges. Two gardeners were working on the far side. Madame Hervé was a middle-aged woman in a bright print dress, and she didn't seem pleased to see me. I asked her a few questions about her husband's disappearance, but she only dully repeated the same things her daughter had told me. She appeared nervous and distraught, and although her features were pleasant, she was fighting to keep them under control. Her eyes were red-rimmed, as if she had been doing a lot of crying. As I prepared to leave, she suddenly said to me: "Monsieur Petersen, the police yesterday were intimating that something tragic has happened to Georges. But he is all right. You will see. He is all right."

I had witnessed that same reaction among people who have been informed that a loved one is missing in action. The awful news is there, but they block it out and refuse to believe it. "I am sure he's all right," I told Madame Hervé, softly.

As we walked back into the house, Celine said to me: "Thank you for being kind to Mama. She is most distressed, as you can see."

"With good reason," I said.

An expression of fright came over her face, and I was sorry I had said that. "Do you really think my father has been injured—or killed?" she asked, anxiously.

"It's only a possibility," I said, trying to soothe her. "There are many possibilities."

"But what possibilities could there be?"

I decided to try one of Inspector Croteau's theories on her. "Would it by any chance be likely that your father is … vacationing with some other person?"

Her nostrils widened in a tiny flare of incipient anger, and I realized how abrupt, and perhaps foolish, my question was. "Impossible," she said, sharply.

"Your mother and father get along all right?"

"I find your question offensive, Monsieur Petersen. My father is a very quiet-living man. Oh, perhaps my father and mother have become a little more withdrawn since the death of my brother. Mama now only likes to work in the garden and read. But my parents are still close to each other. I know my father very well, Monsieur Petersen. We go on trips and vacations together, and I know he does not look at other women. When he is finished with his business at the office, he only likes to come home here and spend quiet evenings."

For some reason, I found her indignation appealing and convincing. Furthermore, I didn't seriously entertain the possibility that Georges Hervé had hidden himself away on some secret tryst. It somehow didn't fit the picture of the man in the silver frame. And even Inspector Croteau didn't believe in it very strongly. I smiled at Celine Hervé. "I'm sorry," I said. "I'm just trying to cover all the contingencies."

She started to say, "But …" and then her features relaxed as her indignation seemed to subside. "I know," she said. "You have your job to do."

Again, my job. Bremmond probably told her that I was an American Government official.

We were at the front door now, and her hand was on the iron knob. "Will you let me know if you discover anything, Monsieur Petersen?"

I promised her that I would, and I told her I would phone her if I obtained any significant information about her father's whereabouts.

"Well.…" she said. "Would you call me at the apartment in Paris? I plan to stay there for a few days."

"The apartment?"

"We keep a small apartment in the *arrondissment seize.* My father uses it once in a great while, but I use it most of the time when I want to stay over in the city. I think I will spend a few days in Paris and see if I can find some more information about where my father is."

"The police are doing a fine professional job on the investigation," I said.

"I am sure of that. But ... maybe I can talk to Paul Bremmond again and some of my father's friends. They may have some ideas ... Oh, I know it sounds foolish. But I can't just sit around here waiting. I get so nervous. I want to do something. Mama will be all right; she can sit in her garden and wait. But I can't."

"When are you going into Paris?"

"Very shortly."

On impulse I said, "I have a car. May I drive you?" I told myself that this was a purely professional interest—the more I could talk to her, the greater chance there was of picking something up unexpectedly. But I couldn't be quite sure that my motives were completely untarnished. There was no denying that this was an extremely attractive girl.

She regarded me silently for a moment again, and then she nodded her head. "That would be very kind of you, Monsieur Petersen."

I waited for her in the study, and to my surprise she was ready in less than half an hour. She was carrying a small valise, and she was wearing a blue shift with silk stockings and high heels. Very nice.

The ride into Paris was uneventful and unproductive, except for the fact that after some initial hesitancy on her part, I managed to get it on a first-name basis. It was pleasant, though, driving through the French countryside with her. And somewhat of an unusual experience for me. Most of the girls with whom I had been associated during the past two years seemed to have been around the track a number of times, but this one had a fresh wholesomeness about her. The blue shift was a few inches above her knees, and she kept arranging it so that it didn't slide up too far; but she was unable to completely veil the sight of a graceful pair of legs and firm, silky thighs.

I entered the city by the Porte de Versailles and then swung over one of the bridges on the Seine to the fashionable sixteenth district. The Hervé apartment was located on a small side street off the Chardon-Lagache, and I pulled my little Citroen up in front of the door and helped her with her luggage.

"What are you going to do first?" I asked her.

"I might go over to the office and talk with Paul Bremmond."

"And this evening? Would you be free for dinner?"

"I thought that Paul and I might . . ." She stopped, and smiled. "I will be delighted to have dinner with you, Monsieur Petersen."

"Brian," I corrected her.

She smiled again. "Brian. At eight o'clock."

I arrived back at her apartment building shortly before eight, and the concierge, a withered old man, made me wait while he phoned upstairs to see if indeed Monsieur Petersen was expected. Celine was waiting for me at the door of the apartment, dressed in a white silk dress and white shoes. She invited me down a long corridor and then into a tastefully furnished sitting room. It all looked very expensive, a typical town apartment of a wealthy manor resident. On a wooden coffee table Celine had set out some glasses, a bowl of ice, and a bottle of Dubonnet, and she now proceeded to pour aperitifs for us. I expressed interest in the design of the apartment, and gently prodded her into showing it to me. There were two bedrooms, the smaller one that Celine herself was using, and a larger one at the end of the corridor, her father's room in which there was a large bed and mahogany appurtenances. It looked immaculate, as if no one had occupied it for quite some time.

We drank two Dubonnets and then I drove her to a restaurant I know on the Left Bank. It is a small place, with low archways that give it a cavelike atmosphere. Each table has a candle fitted into an empty bottle, and the flickering flames throughout the room play picturesquely against the darkened walls. We had another Dubonnet and then a tasty canard, accompanied by a white Chablis. She appeared relaxed, and we chatted effortlessly.

"Where'd you learn to speak English so well?" I asked her.

"At the Sorbonne. And also, I spent last summer in England." Coffee was being served, and she paused while the waiter placed the small expresso cup in front of her. "I think I would like to go back to the Sorbonne again and obtain an advanced degree in English, or perhaps in Spanish."

"Do you want to teach?"

"Oh, Lord, no. I couldn't do that. I think maybe I would like to get enough proficiency in languages so I could work in diplomacy. I'd like to do something at the U.N., perhaps."

"You'd be the best thing that ever happened to the U.N."

She laughed, and then she stopped suddenly. "Do you know, that is the first time I think I've laughed since we received that terrible news about Papa. I feel ashamed of myself—I shouldn't be laughing while we still don't know what's happened to Papa."

"Did you learn anything new from Bremmond at the office this afternoon?"

"Nothing. That poor boy is so confused about the whole thing."

"Bremmond told me that your father has been acting somewhat strangely of late," I said, carefully, taking a sip of my coffee. I tried to make it sound casual.

"Not strangely," she said, guardedly. "He has been working very hard on a big venture. He was very tired."

I decided to use the rumor that Stefan had told me in Washington, and see if I could bluff my way through. "Oh, yes," I said, "that business about the production of atomic power for peaceful purposes."

Her eyes widened. "You know about that?" she said, surprised.

"Oh, yes." A grand slam. Well, at least I knew now that Stefan's rumor was accurate.

I offered her an American cigarette, and after she inhaled the first puff, she said: "I suppose that your people must have information about it, although Papa wanted to keep it strictly out of government circles. It is to be a private venture. Governments can do many things. But Papa was becoming very alarmed by what he called the marriage between the military and the industrial. He was much opposed to de Gaulle, and he often said to me that he was a dictator who was destroying the private sector. And Papa felt that the East-West tension was leading us into a completely military state. And then this invention came along, the one you know about, and he bought the patent for it, at great price. He was so excited about it. He felt that this one invention could change the direction in which we were headed. An international cartel—of private firms in America, England, West Germany, and France—which could produce atomic power inexpensively for use in industry, travel, space, all kinds of things. It would take the atomic power out of the hands of the military and the politicians and place it under private control. And it would make the West what he called economically unassailable. He said that was the way to stop this mad arms race. Through economic superiority, not through the production of more guns. This invention would also supply vast amounts of energy, inexpensively and quickly, for all the people of the West, and thus keep us from falling into another Depression."

"I hope he can do it," I said, drawing on my cigarette. "The good economic life."

"He *can* do it," Celine said, passionately. "If only. . . ."

"If only what?"

She shrugged her shoulders hopelessly. "If only we can find him."

"Who do you think would be interested in stopping your father on this project, Celine?"

The waiter brought the cognac I had ordered, and she fingered the glass, gazing down into the dark liquid. "People from the Iron Curtain countries, I suppose. Or, perhaps even some of the French politicians. My father is not a very popular man with many of them, and they wouldn't like the idea of his stealing their power from them, their economic and military power. And...." she paused suddenly, taking a sip of her drink.

"And?" I prodded. "You were about to say something else, Celine."

She hesitated a moment and then went on. "I will tell you, Brian, something I have told no one else, not even Mama. I did not want to frighten her, and this certainly would, because it has frightened me. Papa told me a few months ago that some people had apparently learned of what he was doing, and he had been so careful to keep it absolutely secret."

"What people?"

"He didn't tell me. But he said that he was going to have to work even harder and faster to finish this transaction. That is why I am so terrified now that something horrible has happened to him."

"Don't worry," I said. "We'll find him."

She took another sip of her cognac and smiled faintly. "I feel better now, talking to you, Brian. I'm glad your government sent you here."

"Well ... as a matter of fact, Celine, I don't work for the American Government, or any government for that matter."

"But Paul said——"

"I know. A lot of people think that, and I let them think it. I'm just a private citizen. Do you believe that?"

She looked intently into my eyes for a few seconds and then slowly nodded her head. "*Je crois.*"

"Your French is showing."

"But why … why are you here looking for my father?"

"It's complicated," I said, and for some inexplicable reason I began to tell her the true story of my involvement in this, beginning with the Ballard woman's visit to my office in Washington.

She listened carefully, but when I was finished, she still seemed puzzled. "I still don't understand, Brian. Why … why you do things like this…."

"It's a long story, Celine," I said, and then I found myself telling her about how I got started in all this. About my marriage. About Marge. I've never told the lousy story to anyone in such detail, and I didn't know why I was recounting it then to this little French girl I had met only a few hours previously. I told it without emotion, and it was almost as if I were listening to someone else relate a case history, but then after awhile it began to get to me and my voice choked a bit. Celine, her eyes tender and compassionate, laid her hand on my arm. "I'm so sorry, Brian," she said, gently.

We had another cognac, drinking it slowly, and soon we were the only ones left in the restaurant. When the maître de began to yawn and make those nervous little gestures that indicated he wanted to close up, we left and returned to her apartment in my car. The concierge was still on duty, and he regarded me balefully as I escorted Celine up to her apartment. At the door, she turned and smiled at me. "It's been a lovely evening, Brian. Thank you."

"Thank *you,*" I said. "What are your plans for tomorrow?"

"I've got to do something. I thought I might visit some of my father's friends in the city, on some pretext or other, and see if I can discover anything new about his activities."

"May I accompany you? I'm pretty good at getting information out of people."

"Yes, you are good at that," she said, softly. "I'd be delighted to have you accompany me, Brian."

She was standing in the doorway, her face slightly flushed, her eyes shining, and I gathered her in my arms and kissed her, gently at first and then more firmly. We held for a few moments, and then separated. She looked at me shyly. "*Bon nuit,*" she said.

"*Bon nuit,* Celine."

The concierge was reading a newspaper when I reached the ground floor, and he laboriously put it down and shuffled over to open the door and let me out.

There were no messages for me at my hotel, and I took my key and went upstairs, feeling pleasantly tired. I snapped the light on and walked into my room, going over to the dresser where I started to empty my pockets. I had just taken a handkerchief and some loose change out of my pocket when I saw it. A small and almost unnoticeable indication, but as evident as a beacon on a dark night for me. My room had been searched. One of the dresser drawers was slightly ajar, and some of the things on top of the dresser had been slightly rearranged. Whoever had done the searching had obviously tried to put everything back into its proper place, although, he should have taken more care to close that drawer firmly.

And then I realized it.

I had interrupted someone in the process of doing a search. And that someone was still in the room, somewhere behind me. In the bathroom. I could almost feel him now. I slowly continued to empty my pockets, trying not to let him know that I was aware of his presence. There was no sense in whirling and charging at him, because he probably had a weapon and he'd use it on me before I could either reach him or get my .38 out of my shoulder holster. And there was no reason to panic at the moment, either. If he had wanted to shoot me, he could very easily have done it all this time while I had my back toward him.

I was an easy target, standing there, and the problem was how to get my gun out and move into firing position before he popped me from behind. I made a quick calculation of our respective positions in the room. The bathroom was directly behind me, but the door out into the corridor was on the far side of the room. No chance there, because I'd have to pass directly into his line of fire. However, the large bed was to my left, and if I could get on the other side of it, I could crouch and fire at him. I finished emptying my pockets, faked a loud yawn, and began to make a gesture as if I were removing my suit jacket. I rolled slightly on the balls of my feet, and then made my move. I suddenly flung myself at the bed, in a sort of dive, hitting the mattress with my shoulder; and in the same movement I kept on going, rolling over, so that the momentum of my dive bounced me off the bed onto the floor on the other side, where I landed on my hands and knees.

I had my .38 out immediately, and crouched low, waiting for my intruder to make a move. There was a moment of hesitation from the bathroom, and then the sound of running feet as he came out, moving toward the corridor door. I raised up for a quick shot, and that quick glimpse gave me the whole picture. My intruder was a thin man in his early forties, black leather jacket, and full mustache. He wasn't armed, or at least he wasn't carrying any kind of weapon in his hands. But he was almost at the door. I lowered my gun and charged into him, hitting him with a shoulder block and sending him banging against the wall. As he came off the wall, I gave him a light karate chop with my left hand across the back of the neck. He went down, rolled over, and as he started to get up again I placed my foot in the middle of his chest, driving him back.

I waved the gun at him, telling him to stay where he was. He was frightened, but he started to jabber away, saying that he had gotten into the wrong room by mistake and would I kindly let him go. I told him to shut up and, keeping the gun on him, I moved over to the phone and called the Sûreté. The switchboard informed me that Inspector Croteau was not there, but they gave me his home number, and I was able to contact him immediately. Croteau told me to stay where I was. He would dispatch a squad car, and he himself would be there in a few minutes.

The intruder started to protest again, and I said to him: "I'd consider myself lucky, if I were you. I was a split second away from shooting you."

He looked at my gun, as if he were trying to estimate how much damage it could have done to him. He apparently felt that it could have done considerable damage, because he lapsed into a sudden silence.

Two *gendarmes* arrived first, and they lifted the man to his feet and searched him. There was a small pocketknife in his trousers, some keys, and a tiny Minox camera with a flash-bulb attachment in his leather jacket, but none of my property. I carefully replaced the gun in my belt holster. Croteau arrived a few minutes later, and when he saw my intruder, an expression of disgust and disdain came across his face. "André Simard," he said.

"Hello, Inspector," the man said.

"You know him?" I asked Croteau.

"Unfortunately, yes. He's a regular visitor at the *Sûreté.* He must have a dozen arrests for housebreaking." Croteau walked over to where the two gendarmes were holding the intruder by the arms, and said to him: "What were you looking for this time, André?"

The intruder started to tell him the same story about entering my room by mistake, and Croteau very slowly and deliberately slapped him across the face. "Please, André, you try my patience. Tell me, now, what were you looking for in this room?"

The intruder shrugged his shoulders. "The usual things. Whatever I could find."

"Do you always take a Minox camera when you go housebreaking?"

The intruder said nothing, and Croteau slapped him again. Croteau turned to me and said: "You must excuse my interrogation methods, Monsieur Petersen. We do not do things as delicately here as they do in the United States." He turned back to the intruder. "Do we, André? Now, please, let's make this easy for all of us. Tell me why you are here, and then the gendarmes can take you and book you, and we might show some leniency since you have no stolen goods in your possession. But if you are stubborn, we will be quite intractable to deal with."

The intruder looked at Croteau and then over at me, and he seemed to make up his mind quickly. Talking rapidly, he told Croteau that he had been contacted by phone to search my room and take photographs of any documents or papers I may have had.

"Who contacted you?" Croteau asked.

"I don't know. A man's voice. He told me what to do."

"And where were you supposed to deliver the photographs?"

"They told me someone would meet me on the street when I came out of the hotel and take the film from me."

Croteau walked over to the balcony and peered down, looking at the police cruiser with its blinking light. Then he walked back toward the intruder and lighted a cigarette, studying him carefully. Finally, he said to one of the *gendarmes*, "All right." And the two policemen led the man out of my room.

"I suppose he's telling the truth," Croteau said. "He's too stupid to invent much of a fabrication." He walked toward the balcony again, and with his back to me said: "For a moment, I thought we might use Simard as a decoy—to find out who his employers were. But if they were supposed to meet him outside, they undoubtedly have seen the police vehicle and have fled by now. Furthermore, Simard is probably too stupid to carry it off."

Croteau offered me one of his Gauloise cigarettes and I accepted it, lighting it from a match he held out to me. "Any idea what they were looking for?" he asked me.

"It looks like a fishing expedition. Trying to find out what I've discovered."

He took a long drag on his cigarette, thinking quietly. "I was going to contact you in the morning, anyway," he said. "Our people have done a very thorough review of Monsieur Hervé's financial holdings, and it appears that he is in excellent financial shape."

"That blows one theory, anyway. And I was talking with his daughter at Fontainebleau today, and I don't think I accept your other theory of Hervé running off with some secret paramour."

Croteau smiled faintly; "I told you that I did not think much of it myself. Also, Interpol informs us that they have not been able to trace the fingerprints of our corpse. They also informed us that they have had some of their secret agents asking their sources behind the Iron Curtain if Hervé has made an appearance there. And the answer is no. And so the mystery continues." He snuffed out his cigarette in an ashtray. "And, Monsieur Petersen, have you discovered anything?"

"Nothing. Except that his daughter told me her father was becoming apprehensive because someone was trying to hinder him in his latest business venture."

"Uh, yes. Well, we will continue our search. But I am getting the uncomfortable feeling more and more in the pit of my stomach that we are only looking for a corpse by this time."

After he had departed, I walked out on the balcony and let the cool evening breezes waft over me. I wondered who had sent that fellow to search my room and find out what I was up to. The Ballard people? Did they know I was in Paris? And if so, who told them? Perhaps it could have been somebody like Jacques Duval back in Washington. On the other hand, the search could have been ordered by someone entirely different here in Paris. Perhaps somebody in Hervé's firm. Or it could even have been ordered by that old fox Inspector Croteau himself, who had to bluff his way out of it when I caught the intruder in the act.

And then I began to think about Celine Hervé.

CHAPTER TWELVE

The next morning I returned my rented car and accompanied Celine around Paris by taxi, throughout the entire day.

It was a wasted effort—at least as far as discovering any new information about the disappearance of Georges Hervé.

Celine visited a number of business offices and then a private home where we had a late afternoon tea, and at each place she introduced me as a friend from the United States whom she was showing around Paris. As a ploy it was successful, and at each place we stopped she casually but deftly brought the conversation around to her father. Everybody we met seemed to say fairly much the same thing: They hadn't seen much of Georges lately, but they understood he was working on some new project that was commanding most of his time. By six o'clock we were both tired and somewhat discouraged. I suggested dinner at another place I knew, but we first returned to her apartment where she changed into a fresh dress.

More Dubonnet, and then a leisurely dinner at a quiet little restaurant on the Boul Mich. Celine was understandably depressed, and I attempted, somewhat artlessly, to cheer her up. She finally laughed when I did my imitation of a New York City taxicab driver, and from that point on the dinner went fine. We walked along the boulevard for awhile after leaving the restaurant, and finally hailed a cab for the trip back to her apartment. She invited me in for some more coffee, which we drank sitting on the small couch in front of the serving table.

I offered her one of my American cigarettes, and after I had lighted it for her, she lay her head back on the couch, closing her eyes. "Oh, Brian, I wish we could find Papa," she said, plaintively.

"So do I."

"Then I could really show you Paris. Not like today."

I was thinking that I undoubtedly knew sections of Paris of which she had absolutely no acquaintance. But I said: "That'd be fun."

She opened her eyes, looking at me. "When we find Papa, you won't have to run right back to the United States, will you?"

Her assumption was that we *would* find Papa. "No, I don't have to hurry back," I said. "There's nothing to hurry back to."

"That's good," she said, closing her eyes again. "We could do so many nice things. Versailles. The Grand Trianon. Maybe even a picnic in the Bois de Boulogne."

I didn't really think I was the type for a picnic in the Bois de Boulogne, but I grasped her hand and squeezed it lightly. We remained silent for a little while, as I continued to hold her hand. When she reached over for her cup of coffee, I drew her gently toward me. She seemed to stiffen and resist for a moment, then she relaxed and came to me. We kissed, lengthily, and when we separated there was a confused and somewhat embarrassed expression on her face. She brushed back her hair quickly with one hand and reached for the coffee again.

"I'm sorry," I said.

"For what? I'm a big girl." She was wearing a green sheath dress, and she tugged at it, arranging it.

"You sure are," I said.

She smiled at that. "I'm surprised at myself. I'm a convent-bred girl, and I'm not an impetuous person, but…."

"I know." I didn't quite know what I knew, but I did realize that I liked this kid considerably more than I had liked anybody for a long time. When she had replaced her coffee cup, I drew her to me again, and she came readily this time. We continued to kiss for quite awhile, and after that I held her gently in my arms, rubbing the nape of her neck. When I unfastened the clasp on the back of her dress, she leaned closer to me, nestling her head under my chin. And, when I started to run my hand across the fine, smooth skin of her back, she took my hand and stood up to lead me into the bedroom.

I quickly threw off my clothes while she lifted the sheath dress slowly over her head. She was wearing a half-slip and a bra in a coordinated design of muted paisley, and I helped her unfasten the bra. Her breasts, like so many of the French girls', were small, but they were round and firm. I helped her step out of the half-slip and panties, and she turned to me, her eyes wide and glistening, her breath coming in deep pulls. I gently placed her on the bed.

It was good, very good. I won't say that Celine was a virgin, but she was obviously without much experience. However, despite my size and the fact I had to hold myself carefully poised over her, it was tender and responsive. And when her climax finally came, her breath emitted in short gasps, and she dug her fingers into the nape of my neck, whispering, "Brian, Brian." Finally, she lay back, her eyes closed, and I rolled over, lying beside her. After a few minutes silence, I said: "What are you thinking?"

"Something I read. I don't know where I read it. A phrase that goes something like this—If you wait, out of sadness ultimately comes joy."

I thought about it for a moment, and she continued: "I only met you yesterday, Brian. But already it seems like a month, maybe even a year. And yesterday I was so sad. About Papa. I'm still sad, of course. But you're the one joy that has come out of this … this awful business."

I put my arm around her. "You're my joy, too, Celine."

She smiled at me, and I think for the first time noticed the bandage on my shoulder, the wound I had received in Chevy Chase. She touched it gently. "Does that hurt?" she asked.

"Only when I laugh."

She seemed perplexed, and I added: "That's an old American joke."

"I read some of the humor in the English magazines, but I do not really understand it."

"Some of it's not very humorous." I leaned over, reaching for my suit coat jacket that I had draped over a chair. "*Voulez vous un cigarette*?" I asked, in the worst possible French accent I could invent.

She laughed and said, "Yeah," in a fairly good imitation of the New York taxicab driver bit I had done earlier in the evening. When we finished our cigarettes, she asked me if I wanted some fresh coffee, and when I said yes she rose from the bed and put on a silk bathrobe with a large flower design on it. She returned to the room a few seconds later, carrying one of her father's bathrobes, and she laughed when I attempted to put it on. It was, of course, much too small for me, and I almost split the seams when I pulled it over my shoulders. The arms came up to my elbows, and it was so short on me that I looked like a Japanese wrestler. But, at least, I was able to fasten the belt.

We drank the coffee on a small balcony off the study, and we had an excellent view of the Paris skyline, with the Eiffel Tower thrusting high into the sky. The evening was mild and pleasant, and the illuminated city appeared as still and placid as a picture postcard. Celine, sipping her coffee, gazed out at the panorama, while I studied her profile. She caught me at it, and remonstrated me: "Don't you like Paris at night?"

"Yes. But I'd rather look at you."

"I have another quotation. And I know the author of this one. Antoine de Saint-Exupéry. He said, 'Love does not consist in gazing at each other, but in looking together in the same direction.'"

"You're a storehouse of quotations. Yes, I'll agree with Mr. Saint-Exupéry, but you've still got to look at each other once in awhile."

She smiled. "All right. Once in awhile."

I remained at the apartment until almost midnight, and after I had put on my clothes, Celine escorted me to the door. We kissed again, and I told her I would call her in the morning. She stood in the doorway, the door held partially open, until the elevator arrived, and when I pulled open the metal gate I turned back toward her again. She blew a kiss at me.

The same concierge had to let me out, and I saw a cab parked at the end of the block and hailed it. I told the driver the address of my hotel, and settled back in the seat, closing my eyes. The whole thing with Celine was happening fast, and I was puzzled by it. Not that I objected to the evening's activities at all. But it all seemed to be developing rapidly into more than an occasional dalliance in a foreign city. I remembered that I was a little uncomfortable about the word "love" in that quotation Celine used from Saint-Exupéry. Love wasn't anything I had thought about for a long, long time.

But then I decided not to analyze it. Just go along and let things take their own course. And Celine was a pretty attractive course to follow. In fact, I had pushed the whole business of Hervé and the Ballard people to the back of my mind. And perhaps if Hervé weren't Celine's father, I'd be ready to drop the whole thing at that stage and concentrate on Celine in Paris. But, of course, Celine wouldn't relax until we found out something definite about her father. For that reason, if for no other, I had to continue the search.

I reached in my pocket for a cigarette, and as I was lighting it, I noticed that the driver was veering left at the Palais e Chaillot, instead of following the Seine toward my hotel. I told the driver he was going the wrong way, but he began to jabber at me about a shortcut and how he had been driving a cab in Paris for twenty years and would I please allow him to do the driving. I knew better than to argue with a Paris taxi driver, and I settled back again, but a few minutes later when we turned left on the Avenue de Neuilly, with the Arc de Triomphe receding behind us, I knew definitely that we were going in the wrong direction. This time I told him, rather sharply, to turn around and go the other way. Instead, he pulled the cab over to the curb and allowed the motor to idle. He twisted around in his seat, a thin, middle-aged man with a pockmarked face. The last thing I wanted to do was get into an argument with a cab driver in Paris.

But then his hand came up from behind the seat, and he was holding a .38 pistol trained on me.

At the same moment I heard a footstep beside the cab, and the door on the curb side opened, and a large man, bigger than I, slid in beside me. He was also holding a pistol. A .45 Colt automatic.

Damn!. They'd picked me up with one of the oldest ploys in the world. The fake taxi routine. They must have been following me around for some time, and I didn't even catch the tail. I'd allowed myself to become inattentive again.

The large man beside me was in his early thirties, and he had a slight, malicious smile on his lips, like a malevolent child who enjoyed torturing a small animal. He placed the .45 directly against the side of my chest, and said: "I am sure, Monsieur Petersen, that you have a weapon. But do not try to reach for it.

We will search you when we arrive there. But if you make one motion now, I will fire this pistol."

I wasn't about to challenge that. His pistol was covering me in the most effective technique possible. There's practically no way to move against a weapon that is held directly against your body. If someone holds a gun on you from a few inches or feet away, like they do in the cowboy movies, then you have a chance to take a swipe at it or make some kind of move. But you can't do a thing when it's against your body, because at the first motion the trigger can be pulled. And then you've had it.

"I'm motionless," I said. I was still holding the cigarette, and the big boy removed it from my fingers with his free hand and tossed it out the window. Then he told the driver to start. The driver put his gun down, and off we drove, the .45 still pressed against my rib cage. I tried to engage them in conversation and ask them what this was all about, but big boy told me to keep quiet. We left the city by the Pont de Neuilly, and turned right. I could see that we were going north on the road to Pontoise. We drove for almost a half-hour through the French countryside before we turned off the main road and began bumping along a dirt road through farmland. We must have proceeded for about a half-mile when the road took a turn, and I could see ahead in the glare of the lights from our car another car, a large black sedan, sitting parked at the edge of the road. The taxi slowed down and then negotiated carefully around it and drew up some twenty yards or so in front of it. The lights from the car behind blinked on and then off again, and my friend with the gun pressed it tighter into my side and told me to get out. The driver of our taxi had, in the meantime, turned off the ignition and walked around to the door from which I was alighting. He trained his .38 on me. No chance for a move here. One gun behind and the other in front.

Standing outside the taxi, the big boy searched me while the other covered me with his pistol. He lifted the gun from the holster, and put it in his suit coat pocket, and indicated for me to start walking back toward the other car. He kept his .45 tight against my back while we walked. The driver of the taxi remained beside his car.

As we neared the black sedan I could see that a man was sitting in the driver's seat, and in the rear seat a man and a woman. Big boy opened the front door next to the driver and motioned me in. As I settled down next to the driver, a tight-lipped young man in his early twenties, I could see that he had a gun, too, which he immediately placed against my side. Lots of weapons around here tonight.

"Good evening, Mr. Petersen," the man in the rear seat said in accented English.

I turned slightly, testing whether the fellow with the gun was going to allow me to see the people in the back seat. He was, and I came around enough to face them. The man was heavy-set, somewhere in his early fifties, and I knew why Henri in the Washington restaurant had been so impressed with his lips. He had thick lips and a swarthy complexion, and he bore a pretty fair resemblance to the drawing the artist had done from Henri's description.

"Good evening, Mr. Hartel," I said.

"Ah, you know my name," he responded, a touch of irony in his soft voice.

I glanced at the woman. I knew her, of course. I had met her in my Washington office. "Good evening, Miss Ballard," I said, "or whatever your name is."

"What difference does a name make?" she asked. I had forgotten how her voice sounded; but, hearing it again now, I found my irritation returning because of how she had used it so cunningly to dupe me.

Hartel said: "I've wanted to meet you for some time, Mr. Petersen."

"You've been high on my social engagement list, too, Hartel. All you had to do was let me know you wanted to get together."

"But on my terms, Mr. Petersen. My terms. I am sorry I had to resort to this form of invitation, but I am very safety-conscious."

"Aren't we all?"

"Has your knife wound healed?" he asked, without real solicitude.

"Doing fine, thank you. How's the man I winged on the street in Chevy Chase?"

"That was bad, very bad, Mr. Petersen. He died a few hours later."

"I'm all broken up to hear that."

Hartel waved his hand, as if to dismiss it. "Just an inconvenience. He was not important."

"And I guess Georges Hervé, whom you killed, wasn't important, either?"

Hartel smiled, slyly. "Oh, come, Mr. Petersen, let's not play games with each other. You know that wasn't Georges Hervé."

"Who was it, then?"

The inscrutable smile again, and Hartel said: "You are my guest tonight, Mr. Petersen, and I think I have the prerogative to ask the questions. But I might say, as a matter of record, that we did not mean to kill that man in Washington."

"I doubt that very much, Hartel."

"Ah, Mr. Petersen. Our relationship will be very poor if it is not founded in mutual trust."

"You inspire all kinds of trust in me, Hartel," I said, acidly.

"When you know me better, you will find that I am most reliable and trustworthy in my business dealings." There was almost hurt in his voice.

"Getting to know you is going to be so much fun," I said.

Therese Ballard—or whatever the hell her name was—started to say something, but Hartel raised his hand, silencing her. "Mr. Petersen, your activities in Washington and this trip to France are proving to be a source of annoyance to us. You received the warnings from our agents in Washington telling you to desist, did you not?"

"I rejected the advice."

"It is unfortunate that you did not follow that advice. Unfortunate for you."

"I'm the restless type."

"You are a peculiar type, much different than we expected." He glanced at Therese Ballard, but she looked away. "However, I'm willing to revise my estimate. Do you see how easy I am to deal with?"

The pistol was still tightly pressed against my ribs, and when I moved slightly, it was pressed even tighter. "You're a dream," I said to Hartel.

He ignored the remark and continued: "We are both getting in each other's way, Mr. Petersen. You are looking for something, and I am looking for something."

"What are you looking for, Hartel?"

"May I again remind you of the ground rules this evening? *I* ask the questions. Now—I thought we might coordinate our efforts, to our mutual advantage."

"You mean, work for you."

"Not *for* me, rather *with* me. I am very easy to work with."

"And what advantage would that be to me?"

"The oldest advantage in the world. Money. A considerable amount of it. You see, I have revised my evaluation. You are much more enterprising than I had originally thought. And you could help me, or you could hurt me. I am giving you an opportunity to help me. A handsome opportunity."

"And who would my employers be?"

"What difference does it make?"

"Iron Curtain countries, I suppose."

"Ah, Mr. Petersen, I am not a politician, I am an entrepreneur. Let us not talk politics."

I looked at Hartel and I looked at Therese Ballard, and I felt the anger rising within me. "And I'm not a politician, and I'm not a super-patriot, either, Hartel. But I wouldn't work with you on changing a flat tire. I might get contaminated."

For a moment I thought he was going to lose that cool composure, but he restrained himself and allowed that thin smile to play over his lips. "That is too bad. . . ."

"I told you——" Ballard started to say, but he shushed her immediately.

"I was saying that is too bad," Hartel said. "If you are not working with me, then you are working at cross-purposes with me, and I must protect myself against that."

I cursed myself softly under my breath, regretting that I had given vent to my emotions here. I should have played him along, pretending that I would work for him. But I had foolishly closed the door on that now. And I hadn't even discovered what he wanted from me. I apparently knew something that he didn't know, or I had some entrée that he needed, and he was willing to pay for it. Dammit. I considered for a moment a change of tack—pretend that he had me frightened now, and agree to work for him. But I felt he was too smart to buy that. And, furthermore, I wasn't going to give the bastard the satisfaction of seeing me beg.

"You have missed a rare opportunity, Mr. Petersen," said Hartel.

"Opportunities come and opportunities go," I said, lightly. I was trying to figure out a move, but with that pistol in my ribs there was nothing I could do.

Hartel took a silver cigarette case out of his pocket, flipped it open, and offered one to Therese Ballard. She shook her head no, and he slowly proceeded to light one for himself. "It is getting late," he said, "and you have refused my business proposition. I am afraid I must leave you now with Gregor. He is very good at eliminating business competition."

Gregor, I supposed, was the big boy, and I glanced out of the car window. He was standing there, the .45 still in his hand, close enough to hear what was being said in the car, and there was a broad and somewhat perverse grin on his face. Hartel leaned out of the car window and said something to him in a language I could not understand. Gregor nodded his head, silently.

The man beside me prodded me with his pistol, indicating that I should get out of the car. And, as I got out, Gregor kept his pistol carefully on me. He turned me around, facing the car, with the pistol held firmly in the small of my back.

Hartel, the cigarette held loosely in his hand, leaned out of the window again and said to me: "*Au revoir,* Monsieur Petersen."

"I'll be seeing you, Hartel."

"I doubt that."

The engine was started, and the driver deftly maneuvered the car around, backing it up a number of times so that he turned it in the opposite direction on the narrow road. There was a steep gully on each side of the road, so he had to work carefully lest the car slip off. Finally, he gunned the engine and they drove away. That left Gregor and myself and the driver of the taxi, who was still standing some twenty yards away beside the car. All I could hear was Gregor breathing evenly behind me, and the sound of crickets in the fields.

We were standing in the middle of the dirt road, and Gregor now prodded me to walk over toward the edge where it slipped down into that steep gully. The sides of the gully were slick with wet grass, and I could see that there were a few inches of water in the bottom of the ditch. Gregor, of course, was going to let me have it, but I had to try to figure out where this psychopath wanted to do it. I doubted if he was going to do it right in the middle of the road, because that meant that the body would be there where someone could possibly find it before they had an opportunity to get far away. I hoped that was the case because if he decided to fire right now, I had no chance at all. That's why I moved very carefully, giving him no cause for alarm at all. He could still shoot me here, if he had to, and then toss me in the gully. I figured that he probably wanted to take me out into the field, far enough away from the road where the body couldn't be seen by a passing vehicle. At least, I hoped that's what he intended.

Gregor shouted to the taxi driver to start the engine, and the driver got in the car and in a few seconds the motor was running. Then Gregor spoke to me: "I think I will use your pistol," he said, and out of the corner of my eye I could see him holding the .38 in his left hand.

"That's nice," I said.

"Into the field," he said, curtly, prodding me with the .45.

At the edge of the road, I saw that the gully was about three feet deep and then rose again on the other side, level with the field. This was the place to make a move, the only move I could possibly make. Gregor had about two inches and twenty pounds on me, and he would be tough to handle, particularly with a gun in his hand. Correction—two guns. At the edge of the gully, he told me to climb down into it. And, as I gingerly put my foot over the edge, touching the wet and slippery grass, his pistol separated from my back for the first time since I had alighted from the car. It was a normal and natural move, since he wasn't going to stay right with me on that slippery grass, but it presented me with the only opportunity I knew I was going to get.

I started to go down into the gully, and I bent over, pretending that the footing was treacherous. It was slippery, all right, but not that bad. I turned, as if to go down sideways, but I dug my right foot into the grass as hard as I could and managed to get a toe hold in the soft dirt. Gregor was standing slightly above me, the .45 in his right hand. But my .38 was only held loosely in his left hand, without his finger being on the trigger. The right hand was the one to get.

It had to be now. I lurched, as if losing my balance, but instead of going down I came up on him, thrusting as hard and as fast as I could. In the one continuing movement, I hit him in the chest with my shoulder and got both of my hands on his gun wrist, twisting it down. The gun went off, but it was pointed downward and the bullet splat into the ground. I followed through with the momentum of my charge against him, grinding my shoulder into him and pulling his arm down. I was lower than he was, of course, and the angle enabled me to do a judo throw on him. He was big and he was heavy, but he came up in the air over my shoulder. At the last moment, I gave his arm a terrific yank with all the strength I could muster, sending him head-first down into the gully. There was a loud snap as he hit the ground.

I scurried down into the gully after him. He was unconscious and there was nothing to worry about from him. But there was still the man in the taxi with the .38. Crouched there, I looked for one of Gregor's two guns. I couldn't see the .45, but my .38, the metal shining in the faint moonlight, was lying on the grassy sloop a few feet from Gregor. I picked it up, and at that moment heard the other man shout: "Gregor, Gregor!" He couldn't see down into the gully from his position on the road, and so I began to crawl along the slick side of the gully, sliding along the wet grass so that I wouldn't make any noise.

I moved toward the area where the taxi was parked, instead of away from it, but I paused to pick up some loose stones and threw them in the opposite direction, hoping the driver would think I had gone that way. I was a sitting duck for the driver if he appeared above me at the edge of the gully, because he could then fire down at me with his .38, and so I kept crawling as quietly and as quickly as I could. I saw a beam play over the edge of the gully, and I knew that he was using a flashlight. But apparently he was exercising great caution about putting his head over the edge of the gully—he didn't know if I were crouched down there with a gun, waiting to shoot if he appeared.

I estimated that I had crawled the twenty yards from the point where Gregor was lying to the position of the car on the road, and so I began to edge my way up the slope to the position where I could just peer over the edge. I was directly opposite the parked taxi, and I could see the driver down the road near the place where Hartel's car had been parked. Apparently, the sound of the stones had deceived him somewhat, because he was walking in the other direction. But he knew what he was doing. He had set the flashlight on the ground so that the beam played out over the gully, making it appear to anyone in the gully that there was his position. He had his .38 in his hand, and he was walking on tiptoes on the opposite side of the road from the gully, listening intently, waiting for any sound. His back was to me, and therefore I decided to steal over to the taxi. He was too far away from me to wing me with the .38, and if I could get to the car I could either drive it away or use it for fire protection.

I lifted myself gingerly out of the gully, and I had one foot on the road when he saw me. He wheeled and came racing toward me, his gun outstretched in front of him. I flung myself down on the road as he fired for the first time and the shell went whistling over my head. Lying prone on the ground, I fired, but I missed him. He shot again, and dirt sprayed up around me. He was about ten yards away, running full force toward me, and if he opened up from that range he'd surely hit me.

I rolled myself over in two quick rolls, so that I'd destroy his aim, and when I came to a stop I opened up. I had already fired one shell, and that left me with five more. I pulled the trigger in quick succession, firing four of them and saving one for the last resort.

He shouted something that sounded like "Awgh," and his legs went out from under him and he pitched forward on his face. I got up and circled around behind the taxi, keeping him in view. His hand was outstretched, and his pistol lay on the ground a few inches from his hand. I waited, watching for him to move. He might be decoying me. A lot of men have lost their lives walking over toward a fallen opponent who they think is unconscious. And that .38 was a little too conveniently close to his hand.

I waited about three minutes, but still no movement. Picking up a small stone, I threw it at the ground a few feet from him, but still nothing. Very slowly, I moved around the car, holding my pistol with its final bullet. I made a rush for it, running toward him and kicking the .38 away from his reach. It was all quite unnecessary. I rolled him over with my foot and saw that two of my slugs had gotten him—one, someplace in the abdomen, and the other under the eye. Since I had been firing from a ground position, my bullet had apparently entered under his eye and then torn up into his brain.

The flashlight was still lying on the ground, and I picked it up and went over toward the gully to look at Gregor. He wasn't doing too well, either. I edged my way into the gully and played the light over Gregor. He was lying curled up in the water at the bottom of the ditch, and I could see immediately that his neck was broken. I had tossed him down head-first, and that snap I heard was the spinal column giving away. His eyes were now open in the vacant stare of death.

I tugged at Gregor's pockets, looking for anything that might be of any help. However, the only identification he had on his possession stated that his name was Henri Larochelle, obviously a fake. No help there. Nevertheless, I made a notation in my pocket notebook of the address at which he was supposed to have lived in Paris, and although I was quite sure that it would undoubtedly prove to be a phony, I still had to check it out. The driver of the taxi had an operator's license in his pocket, but when I compared it with the documents in the taxi, I saw that they did not match. The taxi had surely been stolen for this one assignment. However, I made another notation of all the data I could find.

My immediate problem at that moment was a departure from that scene. I was quite sure that Hartel and Ballard were far from there at that moment, but there was always the possibility that they were waiting somewhere for Gregor and his friend. I would have to hike back to the main road, and then maybe I could hitch a ride back into Paris. Of course, I could always phone Inspector Croteau from someplace, but I decided not to do that. If I became implicated in these killings on a lonely road, there would be all sorts of red tape—an inquest, hearings, and lots of unwanted publicity. I'd let somebody else discover the bodies, and then allow the police to make whatever they wanted of it.

I made a quick survey of the area to be sure that I hadn't left anything that could connect me with the incident. And I observed that my suit was ruined—the whole fabric was smeared with mud, and there was a large gash in the trousers, torn when I hit the ground during the shooting. I played the flashlight around one last time, allowing the beam to fall on the immobile figure lying in the middle of the road, and then on Gregor, bent and permanently broken in the ditch.

I began my long, lonely hike through the French countryside, ready to jump off the road if I should see any headlights coming. But there was absolutely no traffic at all out there in the middle of the night. It gave me lots of time to think.

I knew that Hartel was in Paris with his friend Therese Ballard, and of course, he knew I was here, too. I was hardly flattered that, after trying to have me beaten and killed, he now decided to relent and engage my services on his side. But it was quite significant that he needed my services. He was still looking for something—obviously either Hervé or the briefcase. That could only mean that he had not arranged the switch between Hervé and the imposter. Somebody else had done that and fooled everybody. But the nagging question remained, Who? Maybe Hervé himself. Or maybe someone on the opposite end of the ideological spectrum, someone like the Gaullists Stefan had warned me about in Washington, people who wanted Hervé abducted or killed.

After awhile I came to a main road, and then I obtained a ride in a farmer's truck carrying produce to the outskirts of Paris. There, I was able to get a taxi to take me to my hotel on the Boulevard Malesherbes. But, by the time I reached my room shortly after three o'clock in the morning everything was becoming much more clear in my mind, and I finally thought I was at last beginning to see what really had happened.

CHAPTER THIRTEEN

I slept until almost ten o'clock the following morning.

I reached over for the phone when I woke, ordered breakfast, and then called Celine. I told her, with as much casualness as I could, about the episode of last evening after I left her apartment, and I heard her gasp over the phone. In a flurry of words, she wanted to know if I was all right and whether I had been hurt at all. I assured her that I was perfectly all right, and then made a date to meet her for lunch at a restaurant on the Boulevard des Capucines near the Opéra.

The address that Gregor had in his pocket last evening was located in the Montmartre area, and I took a cab up there to check it out. It was a bum lead. The address was a small pharmacy store, and it appeared perfectly legitimate. I made a purchase in the store, and the old man who waited on me looked absolutely harmless. I even walked around to the alley behind the store, and I could see that there was no back room to the tiny establishment. All this time, of course, I was taking exquisite care to see that no one was trailing me. I knew that Hartel and company were trying to track me down and eradicate me. However, I had one advantage in my favor now—I didn't have to worry about Gregor any more.

I arrived at the restaurant before Celine and selected a table in the sidewalk café area where I could observe the stream of people passing by. Her taxi pulled up a few moments later, and I watched her as she got out, a trim young woman in a pale beige suit. She was wearing black pumps, but no stockings on her fine brown legs. While I ordered a Dubonnet for her, she fired a series of questions at me about my episode of last night. I told her the entire story, attempting to keep as much of the blood and guts out of it as possible.

"And you killed them *both*?" she asked, her eyes wide.

"I had to. Does that bother you?"

"No," she said, slowly. "If they were trying to kill you...."

"That seemed to be their intention," I said, dryly.

"The important thing is that you are not hurt, Brian," she said, laying her hand on my arm. "But did they say anything about Papa?"

"Nothing that we don't know already. I'm afraid that I played it badly, Celine. I should have tried to pry some information out of them, but when I saw that Ballard woman, I guess I lost my cool. Hartel is obviously the brains of this caper, and Ballard works for him. Hartel definitely wanted me to find something for him, and ... it could have been your father, or something else, perhaps the papers he had been carrying."

"But what do we do next?"

"Next? I think we have some lunch."

But Celine was dispirited during lunch, hardly touching the salad she had ordered. The tables around us were all filled, and a large number of the customers seemed to be tourists. Immediately to our right, there was a table of Americans, and they almost appeared to be caricatures out of a *New Yorker* cartoon—bright sports shirts, cameras slung over their shoulders, loud voices. However, on the other side of us was a table of people speaking even more loudly in French. A man and a woman, and two teen-agers.

When the man laughed loudly and slapped the small table in front of them, Celine glanced at them in displeasure. "*Oh, les Canadiens. Ils sont grossiers.*"

"Yes," I said, thoughtfully, and I turned my attention more carefully to the Canadian tourists. They were speaking cheerfully of their trip to the Louvre this morning and their proposed visit to the Palais Royal after lunch. Celine had, of course, immediately picked up their Canadian accents—some peculiar idioms, a slightly different vocabulary, and a somewhat coarser way of pronouncing the French. My ear was, naturally, not as good as Celine's, and my French wasn't that refined. But, by listening carefully, I could now note the difference between the Parisian and Canadian French.

And I began to think of the little man who had been murdered on the street in Chevy Chase.

We had talked briefly in the Mayflower Hotel and then we had a desultory conversation during the ride out to Chevy Chase. Not very much dialogue. I tried to recall some of the things he had said. A phrase. A word. When I had flicked on the radio in my car, he had used the word *le radio.* That in itself wasn't necessarily very convincing, because even the Parisians themselves were beginning to use that word instead of the more traditional *t.s.f.* And when he thanked me for holding open my car door, he had said, "*Merci beaucoup.*" Again, not necessarily a proof that he was speaking Canadian French. But there was something else, something almost indefinable. Maybe it had been the cadence of his French or the very sound of it. I listened to the Canadian tourists at the next table again, and I became more sure of it.

At that moment I felt I knew why neither the French police nor Interpol had been able to trace the identity of the man who had posed as Georges Hervé.

Celine was sipping a cup of coffee, and I suddenly said to her: "When was the last time your father visited Canada?"

"Papa in Canada? He didn't like Canada. Let me see … the last time he was there must have been, oh, two or three years ago."

"Did he have any close friends who were Canadians, people who might have visited your home in Fontainebleau?"

"No, not that I know of."

"What about business associates, that last trip he took to Canada?"

"I don't remember anything about that. But we could find out from Paul at the office," she said, a puzzled expression on her face. "Why do you want to know?"

"I think I may have an idea about where your father is right now. Let's get over to the office." I hurriedly signaled the waiter for the bill.

Paul Bremmond occupied a small office at Hervé et Cie., but it was tastefully furnished with a heavy pile rug and a dark mahogany desk. He rose to meet us as we entered, and I saw him notice, with evident displeasure, Celine's arm entwined with mine.

"Paul," she said, "I'm sorry to disturb you again at work, but there's something we must find out."

"That's perfectly all right, Celine," he said, and I could tell from the way he talked to her that his relationship with her had been something more than a casual one. Had there been a budding romance here? Bremmond looked from Celine to me, as if he were trying to make up his mind about what was going on between the two of us. There was a frown on his handsome features, but he gained his composure quickly and waved us toward chairs.

"What do you want to know?" he asked.

Celine glanced at me, and I said: "Did Monsieur Hervé have any close friends or associates who were Canadian?"

He smiled faintly, looking at Celine. "Monsieur Hervé and Canadians? Hardly. We have done business with Canadian firms, however. There was that acquisition of the Canadian Pacific stock two and a half years ago, when Monsieur Hervé went to Canada himself."

"And that was the last time he was there?"

"To the best of my knowledge."

"What about people here in Paris? Any French Canadians he might have known—even slightly?"

"I am not aware of all of Monsieur Hervé's associations, of course, but I do not believe he has any regular business contacts with any French Canadians in Paris." He paused momentarily. "There was that … that Morrissette fellow, of course, but I do not know …"

"Morrissette? Who's Morrissette?" I asked.

"He is a French Canadian, indeed, if that's what you're looking for. Monsieur Hervé met him in Montreal during the Canadian trip. He was one of the financial people involved in the transfer of the Canadian Pacific stock, a rather insignificant figure in that deal, if I remember. But he continued to write Monsieur Hervé after that, sent him Christmas cards and that sort of thing. An attempt to ingratiate himself with Monsieur Hervé, I think. Monsieur Hervé used to joke about it to me. He called Morrissette that 'Canadian pest.' He was here in Paris last week, as a matter of fact."

"And did he and Hervé meet?"

"Yes, they had lunch together. That was most unusual."

"What day was that?"

Bremmond opened a small leather-covered book on the side of his desk and consulted it. "On the twelfth."

The twelfth was three days before Hervé's impostor arrived in Washington. "Why do you say it was unusual?"

"It was unusual for Monsieur Hervé to have a business luncheon with anybody. He did not like them. And particularly with this Canadian. You see, Morrissette had written some months previously that he was coming to Paris on a business trip and would like the opportunity to meet with Monsieur Hervé again after all this time. Monsieur Hervé disregarded that first letter and did not even answer it. But Morrissette wrote again, more insistently, claiming that he had a stock merger in mind which might interest us, and he would only take a few minutes of our time. He was to be in Paris a day or so before returning to Montreal. Monsieur Hervé finally answered that letter and told the Canadian that he was very busy at this time, but he would give him a few minutes on the morning of the twelfth. At eleven o'clock," Bremmond said, consulting the book again. "Monsieur Hervé told me that he would see the man for two or three minutes and then turn him over to somebody else in the firm."

"But they had lunch together instead?" I asked.

"That is what is most strange. On the morning of the twelfth, Monsieur Hervé told me to contact Morrissette and cancel the appointment, and to tell Morrissette that he would meet him at a restaurant on the Champs-Elysées for lunch."

"And you talked to this Morrissette yourself on the phone?"

"Yes."

"And what did he say?"

"He was delighted, of course. To have lunch with the distinguished Monsieur Hervé."

"And they actually had lunch together?"

"Apparently. I tried to talk about it to Monsieur Hervé that afternoon, because it was most strange for him to have a business lunch, but he just dismissed it and went right back to work."

"You never met this Morrissette, then?"

"Never."

"Do you remember what hotel he was staying at?"

"I can find out," Bremmond said, rising. "Excuse me a moment." He left the room.

Celine said to me, "Brian, I do not understand."

"Wait a minute," I said. "I think we're getting somewhere now."

Bremmond returned, carrying a manila folder that he placed on his desk. "This is the Morrissette correspondence," he said, flipping through it. "Ah, yes, the Pacific Hotel. Someplace in Montparnasse, I believe. He indicated his Paris address in his letter."

"May I see that folder?" I asked, and Bremmond handed it to me. The correspondence was exactly as Bremmond had related it a few minutes ago. The letters from Canada were all written on a letterhead that bore the inscription, *Louis Morrissette, Investments.* I returned the folder, and said, "Thanks. You've been very helpful."

"Do you think this Morrissette had something to do with Monsieur Hervé's disappearance?" Bremmond asked, a puzzled expression on his face.

"Perhaps," I said, rising. "Let's go, Celine."

At the door of his office, Bremmond said to Celine, "When will I see you again?"

"Soon, Paul, soon."

Out in the corridor, while waiting for the elevator, I said to Celine, "Are you and Bremmond interested in each other?"

She blushed slightly. "Oh, no," she said, a little too quickly. "He's just a good friend."

The elevator door opened and I took her by the elbow, escorting her in. "Where are we going?" she asked.

"To the Pacific Hotel."

"You think this Morrissette person … ?"

"I think that there's a good chance that the man who impersonated your father may be Louis Morrissette of Montreal. But let's not jump to conclusions yet."

"But why would he do that?"

"That, my dear, is something we've got to find out."

The Pacific Hotel in Montparnasse was a small, inexpensive place, and the concierge behind the desk was a tall man in his middle thirties with guarded and somewhat crafty eyes. When I asked him if he remembered a Louis Morrissette who had stayed there recently, he merely nodded his head. I then asked him if I could speak to him privately for a moment, but he told me curtly that he was on duty. I slipped a hundred-franc note across the desk at him, and he looked at it a moment before he deftly picked it up and placed it in his pocket. He disappeared for a minute, and when he returned an old lady hobbled behind him and took his place behind the desk.

We withdrew to the far side of the small lobby, and Celine and I sat on an antiquated couch while the concierge pulled up a chair near us. "Do you remember what day Morrissette checked out of the hotel?" I asked him.

He thought for a moment, his eyes expressionless. "Last week. On … on the fifteenth."

Now I was sure that Morrissette was Hervé's impostor. The fifteenth was the day on which he had arrived in Washington. "I have reason to believe that Morrissette met an unfortunate accident and never left Paris," I said.

"Oh," the concierge said, without the slightest flicker of emotion.

Reaching for my wallet, I extracted a sheaf of franc notes and counted out five hundred francs. "There is a body in the police morgue. I'd like you to identify it for me. It might be Morrissette."

"No, thank you," the concierge said. "I don't want to get mixed up with the police."

"You won't get mixed up with the police."

"Aren't you a policeman?"

"I'm an investigator for an American firm. All you have to do is take a look at the body, and no identification to the Paris police. In fact, no matter who the corpse is, I don't want you to say that you recognize it. All you have to do is tell me. Five thousand francs for a half-hour's work."

The concierge looked at the sheaf of franc notes in my hand, and then slowly reached out and took them.

I telephoned Inspector Croteau from the hotel and asked him if I could view the body in the morgue once more, and after he hesitated for a moment, he finally agreed and said that he would arrange for it immediately. Celine remained in the taxi while the concierge and I went into the morgue, and when the body was pulled out on the slab the concierge looked at the face calmly.

"I don't know him," the concierge stated flatly, and the attendant pulled up the sheet again over the corpse's face and slid the body back in.

Neither the concierge nor I said anything until we were out on the street again. "Well?" I asked him.

"That is Monsieur Morrissette," the concierge said.

I pulled another fifty franc notes out of my pocket and handed it to him. "This is for your taxi fare, and to remind you to forget what you saw."

"I haven't the slightest intention of telling anyone about it. I know more than I want to know about it already."

He walked off, hailing a cab, while I went over to where Celine was waiting for me in our cab. As I slid in beside her, she asked, "Was it Morrissette?"

I nodded, and put my finger to my lips, indicating that I didn't want the driver to overhear. I told the driver to take us over to the Brasserie Lipp on the Boulevard Saint-Germain, and during the whole drive Celine watched my face anxiously but we didn't do any talking.

So, I thought, my very original suspicion had been the correct one. And I had allowed myself to become diverted from it by all the complexities in this whole curious mess. But, during the past twelve hours, I had been coming back to it, and now I knew for certain. That old bastard, Georges Hervé, had himself arranged the switch between himself and his imposter, a switch that resulted in the death of Louis Morrissette in Washington. Damn you, Hervé. The only thing I didn't know now was the reason for the switch.

"But I don't understand," Celine was saying. We were sitting at a table in the rear of the Brasserie Lipp. She was sipping a Dubonnet, and I was working on a tall Scotch. I had even managed to get the waiter to put a slice of lime in it.

"It's all very clear now, Celine. Your father switched places with that Morrissette fellow. The Canadian fellow assumed your father's identity and went off to Washington, and your father undoubtedly assumed Morrissette's identity and went off to Montreal."

"That's impossible."

"No, look what happened. Your father was scheduled to leave for the States on the fourteenth of the month. But two days before he is to leave he is sitting at his desk and he sees that he has an appointment with this Canadian fellow he had met sometime earlier. And he remembers what the fellow looks like. Granted, it was only a superficial resemblance, mostly in stature, but it would do. It was at that moment, I think, that your father suddenly decided to switch places with him. Remember what Bremmond said? The last-minute decision to have a business luncheon with Morrissette, something your father never does. This Canadian was trying to ingratiate himself with the big French financier, and I'll bet your father was easily able to cajole him into switching roles for the trip home. He might have passed it off to Morrissette as a lark or something. But it certainly didn't turn out as a lark for the Canadian."

"But why would Papa do something like that? And why didn't he tell me about it? He usually tells me everything."

"Maybe there was something he didn't want you to know this time." There could have been a lot of reasons for the switch, I thought. Maybe Croteau was right after all, and Hervé was making a deal with the other side. Perhaps his honeymoon with the new boys coming into power in France, people like Michel Jobert, was not as rosy as it first seemed. Maybe they resented the old boy, and then he decided to jump the fence. But he needed time to pull it off, and thus the imposter.

"You think Papa is in Montreal, then?" Celine asked.

"I think he went to Montreal. I'm not at all sure he's still there."

"Then we must go to Montreal, and follow him from there. I'm sure he is in some kind of trouble, Brian. He has been gone over a week, and he surely would have contacted me by now."

"I don't know. . . ." I said slowly. Hartel and Ballard were here in Paris, and they were the ones I wanted to get. But maybe a quick trip to Montreal would give me a better angle of attack. After all, I could spend weeks or months in this city of millions of people fruitlessly trying to find them, and as a matter of fact

Croteau and his professional people had been looking for Hartel for sometime without success. But, if I could find Hervé, then maybe I could unravel the whole puzzle in one blow. And then, maybe I could find out where Hartel fits it, and then I could get a direct bead on him.

I looked across the table at Celine. "All right," I said finally, "I'll go to Montreal for a few days and see what I can find."

"No, Brian—I said *we*. We are going to Montreal."

"Celine, you're not coming with me."

"It's my father, Brian, and I'm going to see what happened to him."

I started to protest, but I knew it would do no good. She had a fiercely determined look in her eye. Furthermore, the prospect of having Celine with me was not at all unpleasant.

I told her to wait there a minute while I went to a phone in the rear of the restaurant. I called a number of airlines, trying to get two reservations for Montreal, but there was no space available; the tourist season was in high gear and the planes were filled with people returning across the Atlantic.

Then I phoned one of the names at the foreign office that Duval had given me in Washington and explained the problem about reservations to Montreal. He had me hold the line for a few minutes, but then he was back on the line to tell me that he had obtained two seats for me on a non-scheduled flight leaving for Montreal late that evening.

There was a puzzled, almost frightened expression on Celine's face when I rejoined her at the table. I took her hand and said: "Pack your bag. Let's see if we can find your mysterious father in Montreal."

CHAPTER FOURTEEN

It was early morning when we landed at the gleaming international airport at Dorval, south of the city of Montreal.

Celine had slept fitfully during the trip, her head nestled against my shoulder, but now she looked fresh and spirited. We went through customs rapidly, and then I suggested to Celine that we find a hotel in the city of Montreal where she could change clothes and perhaps take a nap. But she said she felt rested enough, and she wanted to start looking for her father immediately.

"What do you think we should do first?" she asked. She was wearing a blue shift with a tiny strand of pearls, and her dress looked remarkably unwrinkled despite the trans-Atlantic crossing.

"Well—Louis Morrissette is our lead. We should start there. Of course, we're working in the dark. We know that his body is in the Paris morgue, but does anybody else in Montreal know or suspect that? I think it's best if we make no reference of any kind to it. Understand?"

Celine nodded her head. I took our two pieces of luggage to one of those metal lockers and stuffed them in, then returned the key to my pocket. At a public phone booth in the terminal, I consulted a phone directory until I found a listing for Louis Morrissette's firm in downtown Montreal. When I dialed the office, an elderly woman answered the phone and I asked to speak to Mr. Morrissette. She told me that he was out of the country and was not expected back for a few days.

"That's peculiar," I said. "He told me that he'd meet me here today. On the twenty-second. I'm an old friend of his from the United States."

"Mr. Morrissette is in the United States right now," she said.

I glanced at Celine, who was standing outside the phone booth, and she looked at me quizzically. "Do you know where Mr. Morrissette is in the United States?" I asked the woman in the office.

"I'm afraid you'll have to ask his wife about that. She phoned the office the other day to tell me that his return would be delayed, and she mentioned that he was in the United States."

I asked the woman if I could have Morrissette's home number and address, and she gave it to me readily, apparently glad to be finished with the call. When I hung up, I told Celine about the brief conversation. "That's a new figure in the act," I said.

"What do you mean, Brian?"

"The wife. We know now that this Louis Morrissette impersonated your father on the trip to Washington. But who else knows that? Apparently his wife. I think I'd like to have a little chat with Mrs. Morrissette."

We went down to the car-rental area, and while I was making arrangements for the car, I showed the girl behind the counter the notation I had made of Morrissette's address and asked her where it was located. She told me that it was near Anjou, north of the city, and a few minutes later Celine and I were on our way. I swung over near the St. Lawrence River, and showed Celine some of the old city of Montreal, venerable and tradition-laden in comparison with the new steel and glass skyscrapers that were shooting up all over the city. She seemed unimpressed.

"Do you know," I said to her, "that the only city in the world which has more French-speaking people than Montreal is Paris?"

She shrugged her shoulders.

We found the Morrissette home without difficulty, a rather stately brick dwelling in a comfortable residential area. When I turned off the ignition, I said to Celine, "Do you think you can carry off a little acting here?"

"What kind of acting?"

"We need a plausible entrée to Mrs. Morrissette. And we don't know what her role is in this thing. She may be part of the scheme, or she may only have some information about it. Suppose that you pretend you met Louis Morrissette in Paris a week ago with your father. You had lunch together that day. And you told him you were making a trip to Canada the following week, and then Morrissette invited you to visit him. He said he'd show you the city, or something like that. That's all you have to say. We can play it by ear from that point. Do you think you can carry it off?"

"I think so, Brian."

I had to ring the doorbell twice, and I was beginning to feel that no one was at home when finally the door swung opened and an incredibly thin woman of middle-age peered out inquiringly at us. She was dressed in a plain black dress, and her graying hair was pulled tightly into a knot at the back of her neck. I asked for Mrs. Morrissette, and she said that she was Mrs. Morrissette. I presented my card and introduced Celine to her. There was a confused expression on the woman's face, and Celine immediately launched into the story I had instructed her to tell. She did it remarkably well, and it sounded convincing even to me.

"Ah, but Louis has not returned yet," Mrs. Morrissette said, dismay in her voice. "But please come in, come in."

She led us into a high-ceilinged drawing room that had an undefinable musty smell about it. Celine and I sat on two straight-backed chairs, while the woman settled on a small settee directly opposite us.

"Louis will be so disappointed," she said. "He should have been home days ago." There was a note of impatience in her voice.

I was trying to think of a leading question, but Celine picked it up herself. She was really doing quite well, and I was surprised. "Your husband told me in Paris that he would be back in Montreal by the twenty-second...." Celine said, allowing her voice to trail off.

"I don't understand," the woman said, glancing from Celine to me. "In his letter...."

"Oh, he wrote you about his return?" Celine asked.

"He sent me a cable, telling me he would be delayed. And then, three days ago, I received a letter he mailed from Paris." She rose, and went over to a small desk on the opposite side of the room and returned with an air-mail envelope in her hand. I was, of course, trying to determine if her performance was genuine, or if she were merely faking it for us. At the moment, she appeared pretty genuine to me, but I was still reserving judgment.

She opened the envelope and scanned a hand-written letter hurriedly until she found what she was apparently looking for. "Yes," she said. "He will remain in New York until today or tomorrow, and then he said he will come directly home." She turned the letter over. "He mentions here about meeting your father in Paris, and he was so pleased. He is going to do some financial business for Monsieur Hervé in Montreal."

I wanted to see that letter. We were sitting about four or five feet away from her, but I couldn't think of any way of getting the letter out of her hand, short of grabbing it. But Celine did it, and very deftly, too. She leaned forward slightly, a perplexed look on her face, and peered at the letter, as if she were trying to read it upside down. "New York?" she asked.

Mrs. Morrissette immediately handed the letter to Celine and pointed out the pertinent paragraph to her. Celine read it aloud: *I will stay in Washington until the seventeenth. And then I will go to New York until the twenty-second. I must meet someone who is arriving by ship from England on that day. I will probably return home later that day or the next.*

Mrs. Morrissette laughed nervously. "He is being very mysterious," she said. "He was supposed to return directly from Paris, but now he has some type of negotiation which takes him to Washington and New York. But he does not explain it."

Celine was still holding the letter in her hand, and I tried to read some of it from that oblique angle. It was written by hand, and in French, and it was on a letterhead from the Hotel Pacific in Paris. What the hell did that cryptic paragraph in Morrissette's letter mean? For a moment I considered simply reaching over and gently taking the letter out of Celine's hand. But then I stopped myself. I didn't need to read that letter now.

I knew, finally, where Georges Hervé was at this moment.

I quickly rose to my feet and glanced at my watch. "You'll have to excuse us," I said. "I have an important engagement in the city very shortly."

Celine appeared startled by my abruptness, but she handed the letter to Mrs. Morrissette and rose.

"But ... but can't you have some coffee or something?" said Mrs. Morrissette.

"I'm sorry, some other time," I said.

"It will only take a minute," she insisted, looking at Celine.

Celine turned to me but I shook my head. I didn't know if Celine realized what was contained in the letter, but if she did, I wanted to get her out of here. I was now quite sure that Mrs. Morrissette was unaware that her husband was lying in a Paris morgue; and if Celine should happen to understand that, then there was the chance she might let it slip, and we'd therefore be involved in a big emotional scene here. And I wanted to get moving in a hurry so I could catch up with Georges Hervé and wrap this thing up.

I'd have to let the authorities do the dirty business of notifying Mrs. Morrissette of her husband's death.

I guided Celine by the elbow toward the front door, and Mrs. Morrissette followed us, asking us to call again tomorrow when her husband returned. "It will be good to have him home again," she said. "It's lonely here without him, and I want to hear all about his trip and whatever he's doing." She paused, caught in her own reverie for a moment. "He wrote me that he even bought a new suit in London. Imagine, Louis in British wools."

"Yeah," I said guardedly, thinking of the English label on that suit on the corpse in the Paris morgue.

Celine looked as if she were about to say something, but I quickly guided her out the door. I put a finger to my lips until we got into the car. Gunning the motor, I pulled rapidly away.

"Brian, what——" she said.

"We've got to get right back to the airport."

"I don't understand."

"Another mistake of mine, Celine. Your father never came anywhere near Montreal. He's arriving in New York today on that ship."

She shook her head in bewilderment, and I continued: "I think I've got it in focus now. Your father apparently talked this Louis Morrissette into impersonating him on the trip to Washington. And then, your father took off for England, not Canada, as I originally thought. He's been on shipboard for the past four or five days. It explains everything."

"But ... why would my father ask this Canadian to impersonate him? And why did he go to England?"

"I've been trying to figure out the intricacies of your father's mind for the past week, Celine. And he's led me down a number of blind alleys. I'm not going to attempt to figure out his reasoning any more. I think we'll let him explain it himself. In New York."

"Then … then that poor lady doesn't know her husband has been killed?"

"No," I said, softly.

"Shouldn't we have——?"

"We'll have to let the public authorities do that." She seemed unconvinced, and I added: "Trust me, Celine."

Sitting beside me, she gazed at me for a moment, and finally she quietly said, "All right, Brian."

Fortunately, an Air Canada jet to New York was leaving some thirty minutes after we arrived back at the Montreal airport, and we were able to obtain seats on it.

While waiting for the plane, I got a fistful of Canadian coins and made three phone calls from a public booth. I called a travel agency and talked to a polite girl who looked up for me the ship arrivals in New York from England on that day. There was a Cunard liner due to dock at noontime, the only one of the day. It was now eleven thirty and we certainly wouldn't make it in time. But the flight to New York should only take an hour, and then maybe Hervé might be delayed in clearing customs or something. My next call was a long-distance one to Tom Ferris in Washington. It only took a few minutes to put through, and then Tom's voice came on the line.

"Where the hell are you?" he asked.

"Montreal."

"How in God's name did you end up in Montreal?"

"I haven't got time to explain it. I need some help. Georges Hervé is arriving in New York by ship at noontime, and I'd like you to get that New York agency of yours to pick up the trail."

"Christ, I've been through this before, Brian. Am I going to spend the rest of my life trying to pick up this frog at public terminals?"

"This is it, for real," I said, and I gave him the details of the ship's arrival.

"Okay, okay," Tom said, "I'll get Andy Cohen to work on it. I'll call him right now."

"I'm leaving for New York in a few minutes, and I'll go directly to the pier. Do you think you can identify me for Cohen's men? I'll have a little French girl with me."

"Therese Ballard?"

"Well, no. Somebody else. A friendly French girl."

"Aha. You've been up to your old tricks in Paris."

"As a matter of fact, there were some new tricks."

"Did you ever catch up with Ballard?"

"We made momentary contact. It's still unfinished business. I'll tell you about it when I see you."

Finally, I phoned a telegraph office and sent a cable to Inspector Croteau in Paris, informing him of the identity of the corpse in his morgue. I'd let him handle it from that end.

When I came out of the phone booth, I thought I spotted a man who had been hanging fairly close to me since I entered the airport. He was middle-aged and stocky. I casually walked back to where Celine was sitting, and then escorted her down to the flight gate. He sauntered along behind us, a folded paper under his arm, but when we arrived at our gate he continued past, and that was the last I saw of him. After we had settled into our seats in the airplane, I carefully scanned the passengers to make sure he wasn't on board with us. It was probably only my imagination.

However, the man did look somewhat suspicious. Maybe he was only a security officer employed by the airport.

Lunch was served during the flight, and while we were sipping our coffee, I began to wonder how long we might be held up circling over JFK Airport. The sky was beginning to cloud up a bit. But, to my amazement, the traffic pattern was still clear and the plane landed on time. We experienced more of a delay with the American customs, and when we finally had our luggage in hand it was one fifteen. At a car-rental desk, I made arrangements for an automobile, and while the bright young girl behind the desk was doing the paper work, I stepped over to a phone booth and called the Cunard line. Luck. The ship had been delayed by fog at sea, and was now due to dock sometime around two thirty.

When we pulled out of the airport, the sky was becoming darker and darker, and very shortly the rain began to fall, lightly at first and then finally in heavy sheets. I drove as fast as I reasonably could along the Long Island parkways, watching out for policemen. They were particularly tough out there, and I didn't want to lose time by being stopped. Traffic in the city was slowed by the rain, but nevertheless we made surprisingly good time through mid-Manhattan, weaving in and out between the taxis and parked trucks along the crosstown streets. I found a parking place about a block from the Hudson River pier at 56th Street, and took Celine by the hand over to the pier area along the Hudson River. We were just approaching the pier building when a stocky man in his late fifties stepped out to meet us. He had a ruddy complexion and there was ex-cop written all over him.

"Mr. Petersen?" he said to me, and when I acknowledged that I was, he continued: "I'm Quigley. From Andy Cohen's office. There's another man inside near the gangplank. The ship is just docking. Do you want us to stay with it, now you're here?"

"I wish you would. I don't know what I'm getting into yet. Can I get in close so I can observe the subject as he disembarks?"

"Don't know how close I can get you. They're pretty fussy around here. Customs, smuggling, things like that. But I'll get you as close as I can. We could use some help, because we only have a pretty poor description of the subject. I'll see if I can pull some strings."

The private detective was able to situate us outside the customs area with a fairly good view of the gangplank some distance away. About five minutes later the first passengers began to disembark, and I could feel Celine stiffen and become tense beside me. Suddenly, she pointed her hand and exclaimed excitedly, "There he is, there he is!"

Half way down the gangplank and clearly visible even from this distance, was a slight man in a black homburg, bearing a good resemblance to the photograph I had seen at the Hervé residence. Finally: Georges Hervé.

Celine began to shout, "Papa, Papa!" But I told her that he couldn't hear her from this distance, and furthermore we had better allow him to clear the customs area first because he might become alarmed by the unexpected presence of his daughter in New York. Actually, I wanted to observe him unnoticed and see if he were traveling alone, or if he was being met by anyone else. I pulled Celine away from the gate and over against a wall on the far side of the area. The private detective was standing nearby, and I signaled him with my eyes that the man in the homburg was our subject.

Celine was smiling broadly, and I could feel her trembling with excitement as she waited for her father. I couldn't quite share her enthusiasm for this moment. I felt that I knew the trick Georges Hervé had played, and it had indirectly caused me to kill a number of people. However—it had brought me into contact with Celine. I grasped her arm more tightly as her father finally emerged from the gate, hoping to hold her for a few moments more so that I could see what Hervé's next move was, but she broke away from me and ran over to him.

Hervé, walking briskly, stopped when he heard her calling him, and an expression of astonishment and disbelief spread over his face. She rushed into his arms, and he embraced her, still holding a black briefcase in his hand. I walked closer, and I could hear them talking rapidly in French, so rapidly that I could hardly follow it. Celine was telling him something about Washington and Morrissette and me, and Hervé was trying to follow her account with a distraught expression now on his face. He glanced over at me, and I could almost feel his steel-gray eyes probing me, and then back at his daughter again. He shook his head in bewilderment.

I let them talk for awhile, and then I went over to the detective and asked him if there was a room or something around here in which I could have a private little conference with Hervé. He said that he'd find something, and a few minutes later he returned to tell me that he had obtained the use of a small office on the pier. I returned to where Hervé and his daughter were standing, and Celine, who was now somewhat more composed, introduced me to him.

He shook my hand formally, and then ran his hand across his forehead. "Mr. Petersen," he said in clipped English. "I am bewildered. My daughter has been telling me this unbelievable story. I had no idea Morrissette had been killed; there was no notice of it in that small ship's newspaper. But I want to thank you for assisting my daughter. If I can do anything. . . ."

"Yeah," I said sourly. "You can give me some explanations. Straight from the shoulder."

CHAPTER FIFTEEN

The small room on the pier that had been put at our disposal was some kind of maritime billing office. It was narrow and disorderly, and the desk was piled high with invoices and flimsies and bills of lading. There were only two chairs in the room, and I motioned for Hervé to take the one behind the desk. Celine seated herself on the other chair, while I perched myself on the edge of the desk.

Hervé laid his briefcase carefully in front of him, and then took off his homburg. His hair was receding, but what remained of it was brushed back tightly against his scalp. He was wearing rimless glasses, and now he removed them and rubbed the bridge of his nose wearily.

"I have outwitted myself," he said, shaking his head.

"Papa, what happened?" Celine asked, plaintively.

Hervé's eyes, shrewd and penetrating, darted from Celine to me, and I said: "I think I can supply a part of it, Monsieur Hervé. You had Louis Morrissette impersonate you on the trip to Washington, while you went to England and then made the crossing by ship. Morrissette was to meet you in New York and report to you, and after that he was to return to Montreal and resume his own identity. But, as Celine told you, Morrissette was killed in Washington, and the deception was uncovered."

"Yes," Hervé said, distress in his voice. "Poor Morrissette. I have been a fool. Worse than a fool. I have played God and caused another man's death. I met Morrissette a few years ago during a business trip to Canada. A harmless little fellow, and somewhat of an obsequious nuisance. He finally prevailed upon me to give him an appointment in my office and on the day I was to see him, I had this idea, which I thought was so brilliant at the moment. As it turned out, it was a stupid idea. I toyed with Morrissette like a small child with a plaything. He wanted to do business with me. *Mon Dieu,* I did not need his business. But I told him that if he would do a favor for me, I would direct a generous amount of our Canadian transactions to him. It was almost pathetic how quickly he jumped at it. I feel ashamed of myself now."

"He had no objections to the impersonation?" I asked.

"No," Hervé answered, averting his eyes from me. "It wasn't really an impersonation. I remembered that Morrissette was built the same way I was, and all he had to do was make one call for me and deliver a message. To a lawyer in Washington, who had never met me, anyway. I explained that it was a necessary ruse, because of some critically important international venture in which I was engaged. As a matter of fact, Morrissette appeared flattered to be asked. He seemed delighted to be involved in the world of international business, or intrigue, or whatever I led him to believe it was."

"But why did you do this?" Celine asked. "And without telling me," she added, somewhat sorrowfully.

Hervé said sternly to her: "Celine, it is a confidential business matter. I will tell you about it later."

"Oh, Papa, you can trust Brian. He helped me find you. Furthermore, he already knows about the atomic-energy cartel."

"Ah," Hervé said, gesturing in exasperation. "That was the problem—the news had leaked out. And where, sir, may I ask, did you learn about it?"

"From the rumor mills in Washington," I answered, feeling a little guilty, since I had actually pried it out of Celine.

"And Papa," Celine said, insistently, "Brian was almost killed in Paris when he was trying to find you," and she rapidly told him some of the details of my violent episode on the road to Pontoise.

Hervé now appeared genuinely distraught, and he ran his hand nervously across his forehead. "It is worse than I imagined," he said. "I must apologize to you, sir, for the danger in which my foolishness has involved you." He looked from me to Celine, and then back at me again. "However, you seem to have gained my daughter's confidence." He remained silent for a moment, evaluating the situation. "All right. I will tell you. It does not make any difference now, since the transaction is practically completed anyway...."

"The cartel, you mean?" Celine asked, enthusiastically.

"Yes," he answered, "the cartel." He turned to me and asked, "You understand the importance of this venture?"

"I can imagine," I said, and perhaps some bitterness crept into my voice.

"Not important to me as a financial venture," Hervé said, impatiently. "We will make money, of course, but I do not need to make any more money. It is important to the security of the world, perhaps even to the continuance of the world as we know it. It is a realistic attempt to stop the mad arms race. Security based on armament—an unending road to utter destruction! Ah, but if we could reverse the trend and make security depend on economic strength. Atomic and nuclear power are, of course, used in private industry, but the cost is prohibitive. The amount of raw materials required, the scarcity of them, the complicated manufacturing processes. But then I learned, through an extremely confidential source, that a West German named Otto Vliermann was experimenting successfully with a process which would make it possible to produce atomic and nuclear power inexpensively. I contacted Vliermann and told him my plan. An international cartel of private firms in Western nations which would produce and market the energies for use in a variety of endeavors—industry, transportation, even space travel. We would keep this out of the hands of the government, and return the power—the real power, the economic power—to where it belonged, to the people. And the people would be liberated from the growing economic chaos caused by the energy crisis.

"Ah, that is my dream." He paused, and laughed mirthlessly. "But … unfortunately, Otto Vliermann was not so idealistically motivated. He is a brilliant physicist, but also wants money for his patent. I had to prove to him that I could organize the whole project and make a considerable amount of money for him and his heirs. That was all right with me, because the workman must be paid for his hire. But it meant that I had to work very hard and very astutely to bring the whole thing together. And I had to work in a very clandestine manner, too. It was all going very well until a few months ago, when … when …"

"When what, Papa?" Celine asked.

"When two things went wrong," Hervé said. "First, the British began to give me trouble. I was dealing with a British industrialist, Sir Bertram Scott, and he informed me that his principals were not completely convinced of the project and were not willing to invest money until they had more time to study it. Ah, I have had trouble dealing with the English ever since that dictator, de Gaulle, embarrassed them with the Common Market. De Gaulle! Sir Bertram told me that his people would not be able to confirm the agreement until the tenth of this month. And I had to wait for them. There was nothing else I could do about it. And then … then that other problem.

"Somehow—I did not know how—but somehow the details of my negotiations and manipulations began to leak out. I first became aware of it in Vienna some months ago when I was dealing with two firms there. One of the firms seemed to know all about my operations, even small details which were only known to members of my staff. And next, as I knew it must happen, an East German firm approached Otto Vliermann and tried to get him to do business with them, instead of me. They tried to destroy his confidence in me by telling him that I couldn't organize the cartel to give him all the money I promised him. I had to assure him that everything was going smoothly. And I had to work harder. And ... and I had to do it all secretly. Not even tell the members of my staff what I was doing, because I didn't know where the leak was.

"And, finally," Hervé continued, "the major blow fell last week. I received a cable from Sir Bertram on the tenth, telling me that the British needed another month. Another month! *Mon Dieu*, they couldn't have another month. I was about to depart for the United States to cement the final part of the cartel. And what happened next made me frantic. The following day I received a phone call from Vliermann, and, unbelievably, he knew all about Sir Bertram's cablegram. I told him that he was misinformed, and I had to assure him that the British had agreed to the deal already and I was on my way to the United States."

"And when Louis Morrissette walked on the scene?" I offered.

"Ah, yes, poor Morrissette," said Hervé. "I was frantic. I needed time. I had to go to England and see if I could accelerate things there. But I didn't want anyone to know about my trip, because it might get back to Vliermann and completely destroy my credibility with him. Morrissette seemed the perfect answer. He could take my place on the trip to America, and all he had to do was visit the French lawyer in Washington and tell him to postpone my scheduled meeting with the American attorney, Standish. In the meantime, I could go to England and work with the British for two or three days, but I still had to allow them some time for their deliberations. That's why I took the ship across the Atlantic. The five days would allow them enough time, I thought, to complete their considerations. And that's precisely what happened. When I was in London, I had to argue and cajole, and eventually offer them more money than I had originally planned. But, in the end, they said they would reconsider my offer. I was three days out in the Atlantic when Sir Bertram sent me a ship-to-shore cable and told me that the British had agreed to my terms. You see, that was the amount of time I needed, time which Morrissette could supply for me. After he had impersonated me in Washington, I told him to go to New York and resume his identity and wait for my ship and report to me about how it had gone in Washington. I told him to enjoy himself for a week in New York at my expense." Hervé paused and shook his head, sadly.

"And is that why your original trip to Washington was delayed for one day?" I asked.

Hervé nodded his head. "I had to give Morrissette time to finish his business in Paris, and I needed time to obtain a false passport for him. I did not regret the delay of one day, because it gave me extra time to arrange for my meeting in London with Sir Bertram, and it also gave me an excuse to cancel my planned meeting with the American lawyer, Standish."

Celine still seemed bewildered. "But, Papa, why didn't you tell me about all this?"

"I couldn't, Celine. I didn't know who in my office was giving information to my competitors, but I had a suspicion. A suspicion I didn't want to tell even you. And then, last week I was sure of it. The cablegram from Sir Bertram. There was no one in the office who could have seen that but … but Paul. Your Paul."

"Oh, not Paul," Celine exclaimed.

"It has to be Paul Bremmond," Hervé insisted.

I was intrigued by the way Hervé had said "*your* Paul," and it confirmed my earlier assumption that they had originally been more than just good friends. I now listened carefully while Hervé lowered his voice and spoke soothingly to his daughter.

"I know how you feel about Paul, and that's why I didn't want to distress you about this. And I didn't want to do anything in the firm which might give the impression that things were not going well in the organization of the cartel. I had planned, after I returned from America and after the deal was completed, to summon the police and have a full investigation. I now feel that will be painful for you, Celine, in view of your plans with Paul, but...."

"I have no plans with Paul," said Celine, sharply, glancing sideways at me. "But I still do not believe he is a traitor to you."

"We will see," Hervé said, patiently.

I pulled out of my pocket one of the drawings of Alexander Hartel, and laid it on the desk so that it faced Hervé. "Do you know that man?" I asked.

"No," said Hervé, slowly. "Is this the man who is trying to stop my negotiations?"

"He calls himself an entrepreneur. I think he's a chief agent working for some bigger organization. Do you have any idea which organization might be your competitors?"

"Of course. Iron Curtain countries, where the military and the industrial are now firmly and indissolubly bound together. They would love to have Vliermann's patent. And they would love to prevent us from solving our energy crisis."

"Are you carrying that patent with you?" I asked, gesturing at his briefcase.

"Oh, no. It is in a safe-deposit box in a Swiss bank. But I am carrying a copy of all the contracts from the various countries, plus a number of *aide memoirs,* and a description of Vliermann's process. These must not fall into the wrong hands."

"Apparently a lot of people are interested in the contents of that briefcase," I said. "That's the first thing they grabbed when they attacked Morrissette and myself on that street in Washington."

"Papa," said Celine, suddenly, and her voice was full of emotion.

"What, Celine?"

"If you had gone directly to Washington as you first planned, then you would be dead now." She was close to tears.

"I know," Hervé said, sadly. "I had no idea these people would resort to this type of violence. But I do not feel right that another man had to undergo a surrogate death for me. Louis Morrissette."

I took the picture of Hartel from the desk and put it back in my pocket. "You could have asked for help, Monsieur Hervé. Professional help. Much better than Louis Morrissette."

"Perhaps. But I have been used to working alone for a long time, Monsieur Petersen."

"At one time or another, we all need help, Monsieur Hervé."

Hervé remained silent, studying the briefcase lying before him. Finally he said: "I will go to Montreal, and I will see Morrissette's widow. And I will apologize personally for my inexcusable conduct in involving her husband in my problems. And I will see if I can make it up to her somehow—financially."

I was about to make some crack to the effect that Mrs. Morrissette wanted her husband and not any money Hervé might shove at her, but I decided against it.

Hervé tapped the briefcase with his index finger. "But first, I must go to Washington and see Standish and complete this negotiation."

"I want to go with you, Papa," said Celine. "And I want to stay with you until you finish this terrible business." She looked pleadingly at me.

"We'll get you to Washington," I said.

I excused myself for a moment and went out into the corridor where the two private detectives were standing, the one who had met us when we first approached the pier, and his companion, a slight little man with a pinched face. I asked the larger one about the quickest way to get to Washington from here.

He pushed a battered rain hat to the back of his head, and said: "That rain is really gonna foul up the airplanes. Particularly in the late afternoon. It'll take you an hour to get over to the airport from here, and then God knows how long you'll wait for a plane. You'd probably do better driving down. Do you have a car?"

I told him that I did, and then I found a phone booth and called Tom Ferris again.

"Any trouble?" he asked, when I finally got him on the line.

"None at all. I've got Hervé, and I'm driving him down to D.C. right now. Do me a favor, will you, and call Duval at the French Embassy. Tell him I'm going to drop Hervé right at the embassy. The French can take care of their own boy from that point on."

"You sound a little disgusted."

"I am, a little bit."

"What about the French babe you've got with you?"

"Now, that's another story. I plan to give her my own tour in Washington. The Brian Petersen special."

"I hope that French babe knows what she's getting into."

I laughed. "I think she does. I'll give you a call when I hit town. I should make it down there in … say, three and a half, or four hours at the outside."

I returned to the maritime office and told the Hervés that I would drive them down to Washington myself. Hervé rose, put on his homburg, and prepared to leave. "You are being most kind, Monsieur Petersen. I will see to it that you are duly compensated."

"Forget it," I said, taking Celine by the arm. "I've already been duly compensated."

When we walked out into the corridor outside the office, I asked Hervé if he had much luggage.

"No, just one suitcase," he said, and then he paused.

"What's the matter?" I asked.

"Luggage," he said. "Morrissette shipped all his luggage directly home to Montreal, and merely took that one small suitcase with him. I wonder if his luggage has arrived in Montreal yet?"

I didn't answer him.

The two detectives accompanied us across the street to where my rented car was parked. One of the detectives had borrowed an umbrella somewhere, and he held it over Celine and her father. I walked behind them, the collar of my suit jacket turned up against the slashing rain. And I noticed that there was a subtle difference about Georges Hervé's manner now. Gone were the brisk gait and the confident air. His shoulders were slightly stooped, and a sudden weariness seemed to have overtaken him.

CHAPTER SIXTEEN

Traffic was moving slowly across the George Washington Bridge because of the heavy rain, but it picked up somewhat when we finally rolled onto the Jersey Turnpike.

I had offered Georges Hervé the position next to the driver's seat of my rented Ford, but he said that he preferred to sit in the rear. That was fine as far as I was concerned, because Celine then sat beside me. Hervé lighted a cigarette and moodily watched the bleak Jersey lowlands, but after awhile he leaned his head back and closed his eyes. It was the first time Celine had been in America, and her eyes were bright with excitement and animation.

"There's not much to see out on these turnpikes," I said. "Just concrete and centerstrips."

"Do we see any cities?" she asked.

"Not really. Not until we hit Washington." I leaned over and found a map in the glove compartment, and tried to indicate to her with one hand where we were going. "Tonight I'll show you Washington. My Washington."

She smiled, and after glancing back at her father, she moved closer to me, resting her hand on my knee.

I drove at moderate speeds, following the flow of the heavy traffic on the turnpike. We were beginning to encounter the evening rush hour as we rolled along, and there was no point in trying to fight it. Just stay in line and go with it. Celine seemed impressed by the Delaware Memorial Bridge, and she craned her head from side to side as we rode across the high span over the river. Then the Delaware Turnpike, and finally onto the John F. Kennedy Parkway in Maryland. It was seven o'clock now and darkening, and it would be another hour or an hour and a half before we reached Washington. The car needed gas, and I planned to pull in at the next service area. I asked Hervé if he was hungry, and he said no but he would like a cup of coffee.

I slowed down and negotiated the car along the cutoff that led to the service area. After the car had been filled with gas, I drove over to the parking area beside the Howard Johnson restaurant and found an empty space in the crowded parking lot. The rain had abated to a slight drizzle, and the three of us did not get very wet as we walked briskly toward the building. Celine visited the rest room while Hervé and I found a table in the cafeteria. She joined us a few minutes later and the three of us sipped coffee. I was trying to hurry them along, because I felt that if I could dump Hervé off at the embassy and let him get on with his dream of saving the world, then Celine and I could have a leisurely late dinner in Washington.

I paid the check and ushered them out the door. My car was at the end of the parking area, and as we drew near it, I could see that a long black Lincoln had parked beside me. I had noticed the Lincoln once or twice on the parkway, a sleek, easy-moving automobile driven by a uniformed chauffeur with two men in the back seat. Affluent businessmen, or perhaps foreign diplomats driving down to Washington. The chauffeur, in a dark uniform and black leather leggings, was now standing beside the car, casually smoking a cigarette, his eyes gazing out at the stream of cars driving along the parkway. I took Celine by the elbow as we reached my car, and prepared to escort her toward the front seat again. But suddenly something struck me about that chauffeur, something suspicious about him standing there in the rain smoking that cigarette. I wheeled rapidly, but it was too late.

The cigarette was on the ground, and he had a Mauser automatic pistol trained on us.

Just as rapidly, two men appeared from the other side of the car, and they were also carrying guns.

"Don't move, Petersen," the chauffeur said in a thick accent.

I was still holding Celine's elbow, and her father was standing beside us, his eyes wide in fear.

"And now, slowly, very slowly, put your arms at your sides," the chauffeur said, waving the pistol at us. It was impossible for me to make a move against three guns, and furthermore, I had Celine and her father to worry about. I slowly placed my hands at my side. One of the other two gunmen searched me, and he immediately lifted my .38 from the holster. The other one frisked Hervé and grabbed his briefcase, and then took Celine's purse from her.

The chauffeur opened the rear door of the Lincoln, and with his pistol, motioned for us to get in. While we were getting into the back seat, one of the gunmen slid into the front seat, keeping his pistol trained on us. The chauffeur then got into the driver's seat and laid his pistol down beside him. He took a roll of adhesive tape out of his pocket; he reached back and made the three of us hold out our hands while he wound the adhesive tape tightly around them, snapping off the pieces with his fingers. He was a big-boned man with tiny slits for eyes, and he bound our wrists quickly and deftly.

"I have been informed that you are a dangerous man, Petersen," he said to me sullenly. "I am dangerous, too. Remember that."

"I'll file it away for reference," I said.

"Quiet!" he said.

The other gunman was still standing outside the car and he said something in a foreign tongue to the chauffeur. The chauffeur leaned back and reached in my suit coat pocket until he found the keys to my rented car. He passed them out the window to his confederate, who then got into my car and started the engine.

After my car had moved away, the Lincoln backed slowly out and we drove back onto the parkway again. The man in the front seat was holding his gun trained on us. I glanced at Celine and smiled reassuringly at her, although I had very little reason for reassurance. We had been picked up very neatly by some real pros. I wondered where the hell they had gotten on our trail. And then I remembered Hervé's accusation about Paul Bremmond's treachery in the Paris office. If Bremmond was the informer, then we ourselves had given him the lead during that discussion about Louis Morrissette in Paris. All Bremmond had to do was put two and two together and pass the information along to Alexander Hartel. And Hartel apparently had a lot of people he could call on—someone to pick us up when we arrived in Montreal, another group in New York, and this group out on the parkway. I wondered how long they had been following us. Perhaps all the way from the pier in New York. And they had been waiting for an opportunity to apprehend us. If I hadn't stopped for that damn cup of coffee, maybe they wouldn't have gotten a clear shot at us.

We pulled off the parkway at the next exit and began driving westward, somewhere in the general direction toward Frederick, Maryland. After a few minutes the car slowed down, and the second gunman got in the front seat with the other two. He had evidently ditched my rented car somewhere. I strained unobtrusively at my bound wrists and the adhesive tape gave a little bit. I was sure that I could eventually work it loose, but it would take a long time. Adhesive tape is valuable for a quick, temporary binding, but you shouldn't trust it to hold for too long. But I was sure that my captors were as well aware of that as I.

"I hope we won't be delayed too long," I said, lightly. "I have a dinner engagement in Washington."

"Quiet!" the chauffeur growled.

We drove for almost another hour, mostly over back roads, until we were well out into the countryside. I tried to figure out where we were going, but in the darkness I couldn't see any signs. The best I could judge was that we were probably about twenty or thirty miles due west of Baltimore. The Lincoln maneuvered slowly along a dirt road, and finally pulled up at a white frame house two stories high. It appeared to be some kind of farm dwelling, but it looked as if it had not been occupied much in recent years. A green Chevrolet was parked in the driveway beside the house.

We were ordered into the house, the chauffeur walking directly behind us with his pistol in hand. He snapped on the lights and told us to stand against the wall. There wasn't much furniture in the place, only one dusty old couch and a dilapidated kitchen table and chairs. A telephone rested on a small wooden table. The ground floor of the house had one large room and a small kitchen over to the right. A flight of stairs led to the second floor, and I could see another doorway leading to a flight of stairs down to the basement.

Our three captors had a brief conversation in something that was probably Hungarian or one of the Slovak or Slovenian tongues. And then one of them began pulling three of the kitchen chairs toward us. The chauffeur produced a length of rope and told us to sit in the chairs. He worked on me first. Tearing the adhesive tape roughly off my hands, he told me to put them behind my back, and then he wound the rope around the chair, firmly attaching me to it. My legs were tied to the frame, a number of lengths of rope ran across my torso and chest, and my hands were tightly bound behind my back. I watched his technique carefully as he duplicated the procedure on Celine and her father. It was a good technique, because we were firmly bound and immobile. However, he made one mistake, I thought. I would have used separate small lengths of rope to bind the feet and hands. As it was, the rope now ran in one continuous length, and if somehow you could break it at one point the whole thing would come unraveled. But how in God's name was I going to get a chance to break the rope with three gunmen here?

"Now," the chauffeur said, "we wait."

"We wait for what?" I asked.

"For some people to arrive from Europe. To inspect that," he said, pointing at Hervé's briefcase, which was lying on the sofa. "This time we want to make sure we have the right papers. Before...."

"Before what?" I asked.

For the first time, a slight smile played around the chauffeur's lips. "Before we complete our ... transaction."

One of the men went upstairs for a few minutes, and when he returned he was carrying a Browning automatic rifle, one of those dangerous weapons with the long, curving shell chamber containing perhaps thirty bullets that could be fired either in single action or in rapid fire like a machine gun. He settled on the couch, some fifteen feet away from us and trained the rifle directly on us. I turned my head toward Celine and winked at her. Her eyes were wide with terror, but she tried to force a smile at me. Hervé was sitting on the other side of her, and I was worried about him. His eyes were tightly closed, his lips compressed, and his face was a sickly white. I hoped his heart wasn't going to give out.

"Are you all right, Monsieur Hervé?" I said to him.

The chauffeur was standing looking at us, and he walked over to me and slapped me across the mouth. "No talking. You will remain silent."

It was a bad night.

The three of us sat strapped to our chairs throughout the entire night, while there was always somebody watching us with that automatic rifle. They worked in relays, two of them sleeping upstairs and one on the couch guarding us alertly. I tried to figure out the chemistry between our three captors. The one in the chauffeur's uniform was obviously the boss, a big-boned man in his early forties. The other two were about the same age, but they were physically much smaller than he. One of them was fairly slight, and he had a long scar along the side of his forehead, as if he had been pistol-whipped at some time; the other one was a little stouter, but he had calculating, darting eyes, like a trained hunter. However, they both had a competent air about them, and they both handled their weapons professionally. I didn't relish the idea of having to shoot it out with either of them.

And I was convinced that our time was rapidly running out.

Someone was on the way here from Europe. Maybe Hartel, or perhaps even Bremmond from Hervé's office. And I knew what they were coming for. To make absolutely sure that everything they wanted was in Hervé's briefcase. When they had stolen the briefcase from Hervé's impostor in Washington, they had gotten nothing. And I can imagine Hartel's anger when he opened that briefcase in Paris and found he had been duped. They weren't going to allow a repetition of that. They'd come here and check the contents themselves; and if everything they wanted wasn't in the briefcase, then they could slap it out of Hervé himself until he told them what they wanted to know. And after that … after that, they'd dispose of us.

I surreptitiously tried to work the rope that bound my wrists, but it was too secure. I moved slightly in the chair, and it creaked under me. Scarface was guarding me at that moment, and he stood up and lifted his rifle. I remained motionless and he sat down again. The chair was the answer. It was a cheap wooden chair, with the rungs glued together, and if I could break the chair somehow, the rope would come unraveled around it.

Throughout the long night I continued to work that chair with meticulous care, moving it what I thought must be only a millimeter of an inch at a time, so that whoever was guarding me wouldn't notice the sound or the movement. After four or five hours, perspiration was standing out on my forehead, but I was sure I had weakened it enough so that one good, crashing blow would break the chair. My feet were resting on the floor, and I felt that if I could lean over far enough I could raise myself up on the balls of my feet. And then I could crash the chair against something and break it.

But how the hell was I going to do that with an automatic rifle pointed menacingly at me?

I kept thinking and thinking, but I couldn't come up with anything. Celine and her father had both fallen asleep, worn out with emotional exhaustion. And finally, sometime shortly before dawn, fatigue overcame me and I fell asleep, my head leaning down on my chest.

When I awoke it was light, and the chauffeur was standing in front of me, a cup of coffee in his hand. He had removed the tunic of the chauffeur's outfit, and now he was dressed only in the breeches and a white tee shirt. He was wearing a shoulder holster that contained what looked like a Luger automatic. Sipping his coffee, he regarded me indifferently. Both Celine and her father were awake now. Celine seemed in control of herself, but Hervé was biting his lips and he still had that pasty-white complexion.

"You'd better give Monsieur Hervé some coffee," I said to the chauffeur, but he acted as if he hadn't even heard me. "He's going to pass out on you," I persisted, "And he won't be any good when your visitors arrive."

That seemed to make some impression on the chauffeur, because he looked at Hervé and then walked over and held the cup of coffee to his lips. Hervé gulped some of it eagerly, and then the chauffeur held the cup for Celine while she took a slight sip of it. When he came to me, I shook my head. "No, thanks," I said. "I'm particular with whom I have breakfast."

He frowned threateningly, and I thought for a moment he was going to slap me again, but finally a small tight grin came over his face and he said: "You talk big, Petersen—for now."

A little while later our three captors had an extended conversation together on the other side of the room, and at the end of it they seemed to have arrived at some plan of action. Scarface departed from the house, and I could hear the Lincoln start up and drive away. The chubby one with the hunter's eyes went downstairs to the basement. And the chauffeur sat on the couch, the rifle across his knees. A few minutes later I heard a clanking sound from the basement, and I realized what it was. A hole—or better, a grave—was being dug in the basement floor.

"What's that?" Celine said.

"My friend is getting some exercise." the chauffeur answered, and he looked at me, a faint spark of amusement in his eyes. He knew that we both understood what was happening. This farmhouse, I imagined, had been rented sometime in the past month as an operational center or a hideout for this particular job. And I'd be willing to bet that the rent had been paid for three or four months in advance, so that there was no chance anyone would come near it. And now the job was over. After Hervé had been interrogated by the European visitors, we would all be shot and stuffed in the grave which was being dug in the basement, and our bodies wouldn't be discovered for months, if at all. I wiggled slightly in the wooden chair, and I could feel it move under me.

It must have been two or three hours later when the Lincoln returned. The chauffeur rose and walked to the front door, the rifle held ready in his hand. But apparently everything was according to plan, because he relaxed and shouted something out the front door. I could hear the car doors slam, and then voices approaching the house. Scarface was the first to enter, and after him my old friends: Alexander Hartel and the woman I knew as Therese Ballard. And one more person: Jules Giroux, the executive director of Hervé's firm in Paris.

"Jules!" exclaimed Hervé, but his executive director wouldn't even look at him.

Hartel walked over to me, smiling. "Ah, Mr. Petersen, we meet again."

"I wish I could say it was a pleasure," I answered.

"That country road outside Paris ..." he said.

"Yes, your friend Gregor had an unfortunate accident after you left."

Hartel's face darkened. "That was very very bad Mr. Petersen. Gregor was a good boy. I will miss him. Well, never mind. This time it will be different." He saw me gazing at Jules Giroux, and he said: "Ah, yes, Monsieur Giroux is in my employ. Or I should say that he is an associate of mine. It sounds more dignified."

"Jules, why ... why?" Georges Hervé said from the other side of me. "Are you a Communist?"

The executive director, dressed in a dark business suit, shrugged his shoulders. "I am sorry, Monsieur Hervé. No, I'm not an ideologist. It is for the oldest reason in the world. Money. More money than I could ever make in my lifetime."

Alexander Hartel said, “I told you, Mr. Petersen, that I was willing to pay very handsomely for cooperation. Ah, but you would not believe me.”

“Oh, I believe you, all right. I just don’t like your kind of money.”

Hervé looked at his daughter and said to her, “I thought it was Paul Bremmond. How stupid of me.”

Jules Giroux shook his head. “No, Paul is quite loyal to you. He has one defect, however. He is a little naïve, and he talks too much. At least, he talks too much to me. And——”

Hartel snapped his fingers suddenly. “We are wasting time,” he said. “The briefcase.”

The briefcase was handed to him, and he took it over to the kitchen table, where he flipped it open and began pulling out papers. He motioned for Jules Giroux, who then sat down at the table and put on a pair of dark-rimmed glasses. Giroux began to study the papers carefully, turning over the pages, while Hartel stood behind him, looking over his shoulder. Therese Ballard lighted a cigarette, and she looked contemptuously at me, a slight smirk on her face.

“You’re mixed up with some great people,” I said to her.

However, the chauffeur, who was still holding the rifle, stepped in front of me and waved the barrel in my face. “No more talking,” he growled.

The sound of digging was still going on beneath us in the basement.

Jules Giroux studied the contents of Hervé’s briefcase for about half an hour until he finally said to Hartel, “It is all there.”

“No questions?” Hartel asked him.

“No questions.”

Hartel smiled broadly. “Then we have completed our assignment. And our work here is through.” He consulted his watch.

"If we drive right back to the airport, perhaps we can catch an evening flight to Europe." He said something to the chauffeur, and the chauffeur nodded and handed the rifle to Scarface. The chauffeur got his uniform tunic and put it on, and began to button up the front of it.

Hartel turned to me. "*Au revoir,* Mr. Petersen."

"Okay, Hartel, you've got what you want," I said, "why don't you let Hervé and his daughter go now. They haven't done anything to you."

Hartel looked at Hervé and Celine, and he shook his head sadly. "Yes, I know. It is unfortunate. But things have gone too far now. They would be able to identify us," he said, waving his hand, "and it would only complicate things. It is better this way."

"You son of a bitch!" I said.

"Ah, Mr. Petersen, do not lose your temper. Your last moments of life should be peaceful. It will not hurt, I assure you."

I looked at Celine, and her eyes were wide with terror. She now realized that they were going to kill us.

The chauffeur went out and started the Lincoln, and Hartel moved the rest of the group toward the door. At the last moment, he paused and looked back at me, a thin, vicious smile on his lips. Scarface, who was holding the rifle, was standing in the doorway with Hartel, and as the group started toward the car, Scarface walked with them, talking with Hartel. For the first time, we were alone and unguarded in the room. The chubby one was downstairs, digging away, and Scarface was probably about ten or fifteen feet outside the front door.

This had to be the moment.

I rocked myself forward on the chair and managed to get up on the balls of my feet, like a hunchback carrying a great weight on his back. The chair was about two or three feet away from the wall behind me, and with a lunge backward I could probably slam it into the wall and break the frame of the chair. But Scarface was still too close. He'd hear the noise and come running in here before I could extricate myself.

Go on, I told him, *walk down to the car with Hartel. Tell him what a great guy he is. Ingratiate yourself with him.* I could hear Hartel and Scarface talking, and then Hartel laughed. And as if Scarface had heard my promptings, he began to walk with Hartel toward the car.

Celine and her father were watching me apprehensively, and I whispered to Hervé, "Look out the window. See where they're standing."

Hervé, who had a better angle out the window than I did, said, "They're all standing beside the car."

I poised, flexed myself, and prepared to slam the chair back against the wall. I wanted to do it with enough force to break it, but with as little noise as possible. I rocked once, and jammed the chair back. It hit the wall with a thud, creaked weirdly for a moment, but held. Goddamnit. I inched the chair away from the wall, bouncing it along the floor, and got set to drive again.

"Hurry," Hervé whispered.

I drove backwards, slamming it harder this time, and there was a sharp crack as the frame snapped. I went down on the floor, the demolished chair under me, and I began to pull my hands out of the loosened ropes. I got them free and jerked the rest of the rope off my legs, and stood up.

CHAPTER SEVENTEEN

I whispered to Hervé, "Did they hear anything out there?"

"No, no," he said. "They're still there."

But apparently the one in the basement heard something, because the clank of the shovel stopped suddenly down there and I could hear him coming up the stairs. I picked up the biggest piece of the demolished chair and went over and flattened myself against the wall next to the door frame leading to the basement steps. He came into the room, his pistol drawn, and he started to say, "What?" as he saw the broken chair and scattered rope, but I brought the piece of wood down on his gun hand and in the same motion hit him furiously in the groin with my knee. As he came toward me, I grabbed him around the throat and squeezed with full pressure. His eyes bulged and he tried to get my hands off his neck, but in a few seconds he went limp, falling into my arms. I let him go, hitting him with a karate chop as he went down, so that he'd stay out for a good while.

I picked up his pistol, a Colt .45, and darted over to the window. Crouching beneath the frame, I peered cautiously over it. Everybody was in the car now, except Scarface with the rifle. Good. Let them all drive away, and I'd only have Scarface to contend with. *Just stay there until the car pulls off, Scarface. Say good-by to your buddy Hartel.*

Keeping low, I ran over to the phone and picked it up. It was a rural line, without a dial, and I had to wait until the operator came on the line. When she answered, I said: "This is an emergency. A kidnaping. Send all the cops you can. State police, everything."

There was a gasp, and then she said: "Where are you?

"I don't know. I'm going to leave this line open so you can trace it."

I put the receiver on the floor and went back to the window again. Everything was fine. The car was almost ready to leave, and Scarface was still there. I crawled over to Celine's chair and began to unfasten her. The knots were tight, and I had to yank savagely at them to release her. I told her to untie her father, and I crawled back to the window again, the .45 in my hand. Damn. Scarface had left the car and was now halfway up the front walk, returning to the house. Slowly, the car began to move away. Just a few more seconds, that's all I needed. *Let that car get the hell out of here.* The car was moving, and Scarface was almost at the front door. It was going to be close. I could fire out the window now and hit Scarface, but they'd hear it in the car. I had to wait.

Scarface only walked halfway through the front door when he saw what had happened. He shouted loudly and swung the rifle around at me, but I fired instantly. Crouched beside the window, I had a bad angle, and my bullet ricocheted off the doorframe. Scarface went running away from the house, shouting, and I tried to hit him from the window, but I missed again. The Lincoln was about fifty yards up the road, but now it stopped, and a few seconds later it turned around and came zooming back. When it stopped in front of the house, I fired at it, but all the occupants scrambled out of the opposite side of the car. The rifle began firing at the house, and glass from the windows shattered around me.

"Keep down!" I told Hervé and Celine. "And stay away from the windows."

Hervé squatted against the wall, while Celine crawled over near me. I pushed her down on the floor beside me, and I thought—with complete irrelevance—that her dress was now a complete mess. She had worn it from Paris to Montreal to New York to here, and now it was torn and wrinkled, and there were runs in both her stockings.

A barrage of bullets pounded the house, and I lay low until it stopped. Then I took a quick look over the window sill and fired at the Lincoln once more. In that one glance I could see that they were all still standing behind the car, firing at the house with their hand weapons. The automatic rifle was off to the right behind a tree. I turned the .45 over in my hand, and pulling open the cartridge chamber, counted my remaining bullets. Four. That wasn't enough.

And Hartel and his friends were smart enough to realize that they had to get to me quickly. They were aware of the fact that there was a telephone in the house and that I had undoubtedly called for help. Time was running out for them, too. They had to finish us off and get out of here. But I had the house, and I had a gun. They would have to make the first move.

It was silent for almost a minute, and I didn't know what they were planning. Cautiously, I peered over the windowsill again, and I could see them moving away from the car at some distance behind it, probably to take up positions on various sides of the house. With the exception of Jules Giroux, they probably all had guns, and I was going to be surrounded by massive firepower. Sure enough. A few seconds later a deafening barrage opened, and bullets began crashing through the windows from all sides. Then, an ominous silence again. I heard a loud voice shouting, and when I peered over the windowsill I saw the chauffeur rushing at the house, the Luger firing in his hand. He was running a zigzag pattern, and he kept darting between trees so that I couldn't get a clear shot at him. But he kept coming, and in a few seconds he would be beyond the last tree, and I'd let him have it when he got in the open. I lay the pistol on the windowsill, steadying my aim, but when the chauffeur reached the last tree he suddenly crouched behind it.

And I realized what it was.

A fake, diversionary rush.

The real rush was coming from some other direction. I twisted around, bringing my gun around with me, and I was firing at the very instant the back door crashed open. Scarface came in on a run, the Browning automatic in his hands, the trigger pressed down and bullets splattering all around me. I think it was my second bullet that got him. At one moment his face was white and tense and grim, and the next it was all red and distorted. He pitched forward on his face, the rifle bouncing away from him. Celine whimpered beside me, and she leaned over, clutching her leg. I pulled her hand away, and I saw that she had been hit in the thigh. A clean wound, the bullet had gone right through. Her hair was down over her face and I couldn't see her eyes, but she said to me in a hoarse whisper, "Go on, Brian. Stop them."

I saw that Hervé, sitting terrified on the floor, was unhit, and I threw my .45 over at him. "Cover it from here," I said. "I'll be right back."

I scooped up the automatic rifle, and it felt comforting in my hands. Running at full speed, I went out the back door, bent over low. But there was nobody else at the rear of the house. They had apparently split up so that the chauffeur took the front and Scarface, the back. But that still left Hartel and Ballard and Giroux unaccounted for. Stealthily, I moved over to the corner of the building and peeked around to the driveway beside the house. The green Chevrolet was still parked there, and behind it Hartel and Therese Ballard. Hartel and I saw each other instantly, and as he raised his revolver to fire, I opened up with the automatic. He and Ballard crouched behind the car as my bullets went thudding into it.

Now it was my turn for a rush. I went at them in a full run, and in combat position. Zigzag pattern, bent over low, my finger squeezed on the trigger, and my left hand across the barrel of the rifle so that it wouldn't rise on me. I came around the side of the car, and Hartel turned to fire at me. But my automatic, operating like a machine gun, was firing rapid action and my bullets caught him right in the chest. He went over on his side, slowly, like he was being let down gently by wires. Therese Ballard had been standing behind him, some kind of little silver pistol in her hand, and she was wiggling it at me, trying to get a shot off. Without releasing my finger from the trigger, I brought the automatic up and caught her someplace in the abdomen. She must have taken four or five bullets before she went down.

I stepped over the bodies and positioned myself at the rear fender of the car, gazing out toward the front of the house to find out what the chauffeur was doing. He had apparently heard the shots at the side of the house, and now he came charging around the corner, the Luger in his hand. From my position behind the car, I opened fire. I used the technique they teach you in the training manuals for the use of automatic weapons—when you're firing at a moving object, hit the ground in front of it and then raise your gun, bringing the stream of bullets up into the object. My first bullets smacked into the ground about ten yards in front of the chauffeur, sending up puffs of dirt and dust, and I raised the rifle, sending the trail of bullets streaking directly at him, like a shark moving relentlessly toward its prey. He knew he was caught, and he stopped instantly, throwing his gun away from him. "Stop, stop!" he shouted.

I almost didn't stop, but when my train of bullets reached a few feet in front of him, I caught myself and released the trigger. I walked over to him and turned him around, and with my rifle in his back, I marched him over to the other side of the house. Jules Giroux was over there someplace. As we came around the corner of the building, the chauffeur first and myself with the rifle in his back, I could see Giroux standing some twenty or thirty yards back from the house, a pistol in his hand. It was obvious that he didn't know how to use it. Hartel or somebody had pressed it into his hand, and told him to go over there and fire at the building. I told him to drop the gun, and he did—almost eagerly.

There was a short length of rope lying in the yard, and I made the chauffeur tie up Jules Giroux while I kept him covered with the rifle. When he had finished tying Giroux's hands, he turned toward me, and I hit him along the side of the head with the butt of my rifle. I found another piece of rope and tied his hands.

At that moment, I heard the distant sound of a siren moving toward us.

I went back into the house, the rifle still in my hands, but when I entered the room, there was something wrong. Hervé was sitting on the floor holding Celine's head in his lap, and there was a strange stiffness about her. I dropped the rifle and went running over. Hervé looked up at me, an agonized look on his face. The upper part of Celine's blue dress was saturated with red blood.

"What happened?" I asked.

"That maniac," Hervé said, nodding toward the door through which Scarface had come charging in, "shot her in the chest. I didn't know it until after you went out that door. When she straightened up, the blood all started to pour out, and then she fell over."

I looked at Celine's face. It was twisted and strained, but still quite beautiful in death.

I'm a little confused about what happened the next few hours. I remember the arrival of the first police car, and then after that there were a hell of a lot of police cars and officers. I do remember phoning Tom Ferris in Washington, and he got up there in a few hours, bringing Duval from the French Embassy with him. Some FBI people also came.

They took the chauffeur and Jules Giroux and the chubby gunman away fairly quickly, but there was a lot of red tape about all the bodies—Hartel, and Ballard, and Scarface. And, of course, Celine. Hervé really went to pieces, and he didn't want to leave Celine's body lying there with a sheet over it, but Duval finally persuaded him to return to the embassy in Washington, where he could complete his business and return to Paris the next day. I promised Hervé that I'd get her body on a plane that very day.

There was a lot of crap about an autopsy and a coroner's report, but somebody—I don't know who it was, maybe Ferris or Duval or even the FBI guys—opened some doors and a quick autopsy was arranged in Baltimore. Tom drove me into Baltimore in his car, and I went to an undertaker's where I made arrangements for a quick embalming. There wasn't any flight from Friendship Airport to Paris that evening, but I was able to make reservations for the casket to be flown to London and then transferred directly to a Paris flight.

At that point, Tom tried to encourage me to return to Washington with him, but I told him I was going to wait until I saw that body on the plane. I was getting pretty truculent, and I guess Tom decided to play along with me. I even insisted on riding in the front seat of the hearse out to the airport, while Tom followed behind in his car.

They didn't want to allow us to accompany the casket out to the plane. Regulations, or something like that. But Tom talked to some people and flashed some cards, and they let us follow it out on the tarmac where the big British jet was parked. I watched the airline personnel in the white coveralls lift the casket slowly up into the body of the plane. And we waited there until it took off. The engines started with that thunderous jet noise, and the wind whipped all around us as the plane moved out to its starting position on the runway. It stood there for perhaps five minutes until it began to roll down the concrete strip, faster and faster, finally rising into the sky. I watched it until it disappeared from view.

"Okay," Tom said, gently, taking me by the arm.

Tom drove me back to Washington, and he asked me if I'd like to come to his house for supper. But I told him I'd rather be alone tonight. When he let me off in front of my house in Virginia, I said, "Thanks, Tom. I appreciate it."

"I'll call you in the morning."

"Sure."

I went through the darkened house, turning on lights. I wasn't there more than five minutes when the phone rang. It was Joyce, my divorcee friend from down the road.

"Where've you been?" she asked, cheerfully. "I've been calling you for days."

"I had to go out of the country, Joyce. On business."

"Where'd you go?"

"Lots of places. Paris, mainly."

"Oo, la la. That sounds romantic."

"Listen, Joyce, I just walked in the front door, and I'm pretty tired. I haven't had supper yet."

"Want me to come over and cook for you? I've got the kids all battened down."

"Oh, I'm just going to have a little something and fall right into bed. I'm bushed. Some other night, honey."

After I hung up I went into the kitchen and looked in the deep freeze. There were all sorts of things there, but despite the fact that I hadn't eaten in God knows how many days, I wasn't hungry at all. I poured myself a Scotch, and cut a piece of lime and plopped it into the glass. Carrying the glass, I walked out to the pool area and sat on one of the patio chairs.

Summer was waning, and there was a mild breeze in the air, and I sat there sipping my drink, thinking about these last few horrible days. I still had a lingering doubt that somehow Jacques Duval was mixed up in this someplace, but at the moment there was nothing I could prove. I could always work on that later. Anyway, I had gotten Hartel and Ballard, and they were the big ones.

But all I could really think about now was Celine. Awwh, goddamn. Finally, I noticed that my drink was empty, and I extracted the piece of lime from the glass. I held it in my hand for a few seconds, and then I tossed it into the pool. It hit the water, floated buoyantly for a moment, until it finally disappeared beneath the surface.

www.ingramcontent.com/pod-product-compliance
Lightning Source LLC
Chambersburg PA
CBHW030824020726
47499CB00006B/2061
* 9 7 8 1 9 5 4 8 4 1 9 4 9 *